"There have been two deaths of Israelis recently, thousands of miles apart, but they tied into something much bigger," Smith said. "Both victims were involved in the nuclear area. We have reason to believe that these deaths may signal an impending attack on a recent addition to the Israeli armament."

Remo waved a hand in front of his face as if shooing a fly away. "Run that by me again. This time, try English."

"These violent incidents might be directly related to a stockpile of powerful armaments that might threaten the entire world."

"I got it," Remo said, snapping his fingers. "You're talking about atomic bombs. He's talking about atomic bombs, Chiun," he called.

"Shhh," said Chiun in a loud voice. "If the Emperor wishes to talk about atomic bombs, I alone will protect his right to do so. Go ahead, great one, and speak of atomic bombs in perfect safety. But where do we go from here?"

"Israel," said Smith. "This might be a prelude to World War III. The two dead men had been involved with atomic weapons. With terrorists running wild there, who knows what might be going on? Any kind of incident could blow up the Middle East. Perhaps the whole world."

Their next stop would be the Holy Land—and when they were through—a holy mess!

THE DESTROYER
By Warren Murphy and Richard Sapir

#1:	CREATED, THE DESTROYER	(17-036-7, $3.50)
#2:	DEATH CHECK	(17-037-5, $3.50)
#3:	CHINESE PUZZLE	(17-038-3, $3.50)
#4:	MAFIA FIX	(17-039-1, $3.50)
#5:	DR. QUAKE	(17-040-5, $3.50)
#6:	DEATH THERAPY	(17-041-3, $3.50)
#7:	UNION BUST	(17-144-4, $3.50)
#8:	SUMMIT CHASE	(17-145-2, $3.50)
#9:	MURDER'S SHIELD	(17-146-0, $3.50)
#10:	TERROR SQUAD	(17-147-9, $3.50)
#11:	KILL OR CURE	(17-148-7, $3.50)
#12:	SLAVE SAFARI	(17-149-5, $3.50)
#13:	ACID ROCK	(17-195-9, $3.50)
#14:	JUDGEMENT DAY	(17-196-7, $3.50)
#15:	MURDER WARD	(17-197-5, $3.50)
#16:	OIL SLICK	(17-198-3, $3.50)
#17:	LAST WAR DANCE	(17-199-1, $3.50)
#18:	FUNNY MONEY	(17-200-9, $3.50)

Available wherever paperbacks are sold, or order direct from the Publisher. Send cover price plus 50¢ per copy for mailing and handling to Pinnacle Books, Dept. 17-295, 475 Park Avenue South, New York, N.Y. 10016. Residents of New York, New Jersey and Pennsylvania must include sales tax. DO NOT SEND CASH.

The #27 Destroyer

WARREN MURPHY & RICHARD SAPIR

THE LAST TEMPLE

PINNACLE BOOKS
WINDSOR PUBLISHING CORP.

PINNACLE BOOKS

are published by

Windsor Publishing Corp.
475 Park Avenue South
New York, NY 10016

Copyright © 1977 by Richard Sapir and Warren Murphy

All rights reserved. No part of this book may be reproduced in any form or by any means without the prior written consent of the Publisher, excepting brief quotes used in reviews.

Fifth printing: December, 1989

Printed in the United States of America

For Ric, Melissa, and the glorious House of Sinanju (American drop P. O. Box 1149, Pittsfield, Mass. 01201).

THE LAST TEMPLE

CHAPTER ONE

Ben Isaac Goldman separated them, cold and thin, then stuck them into their stainless steel cages and lowered them into the boiling grease and watched them fry.

Then he watched the frozen golden chunks in their pale dough coffins being lowered alongside into the earth of liquid grease.

The next day Ben Isaac supervised the grilling of the round, flat pieces of meat, which were USDA inspected and not more than 27 percent fat. When the red light flashed and the buzzer sounded, he would automatically turn them over and sprinkle salt onto their burned backs. As they sizzled and spat at him from the grill, he would lower the solid weight atop them to keep them pressed down flat.

The day after that had always been Ben Isaac's favorite. He lined them up, bread round, acned with sesame seed, then fed them into the ovens.

After they were done, he would wrap them in their colorful paper shrouds and stick them in their styrofoam coffins.

For nearly two years, this daily, rhythmic eight-hour massacre had brought Ben Isaac Goldman a certain cleansing peace.

For two years, he had changed symbols: he had traded the six million dead from the swastika for the twenty billion sold from the golden arches. And he was content.

But no longer. He had lost his faith in both symbols, the swastika for which he had worked thirty years earlier, and the golden arches, which he served as an assistant manager in Baltimore, Maryland, spending three days a week controlling the scientifically designed slaughter of helpless food stuffs.

And so now he just went through the motions, his small paper cap squashed down on his wispy white curls, shuffling in greasy black shoes from section to section, making sure the plastic, non-dairy shakes weighed enough, that the measured-before-cooking semiburgers were not in their waiting bins more than seven minutes, and that the onion, tomato, pickle, and special sauce bins were never less than half full.

And he waited only for the end of his workday when he could take off the cheap white gloves he bought each day in Walgreen's drugstore, and drop them into the garbage on his way out.

Recently, he had taken to washing his hands constantly.

On a Sunday evening in April, a spring that promised a bone-melting hot summer, Ben Isaac Goldman pushed open the swinging top of the garbage can in front of the hamburger store, and watched as someone else dropped a pair of white gloves in. He followed with his own gloves, then looked up and met for the first time Ida Bernard, a tight-boned middle-aged lady, originally from the Bronx, who worked at the ice cream place next door.

She wore white gloves too, because her hands got cold working with the soft ice cream so many hours a day, making Mother's Day cakes and birthday treats and sundaes and flying saucers and parfaits and simple plastic cones, all under the auspices of an old man who did his own television commercials and sounded like a candidate for a total laryngectomy.

Besides their use of gloves, Ben and Ida suddenly discovered, talking over the trashcan, that they had a lot of other things in common. Like they both hated hamburgers. And they both hated ice cream. And weren't prices awful nowadays? And wasn't summer going to be hot this year? And why didn't they continue this scintillating conversation over dinner?

So at 8:30 on a Sunday night, Ben Isaac Goldman and Ida Bernard went off in search of a restaurant that did not feature either hamburgers or ice cream.

"I love good peas and carrots, don't you?" asked Ida, who had taken Ben Isaac's arm. She was taller than he was and thinner, but they both had the same length stride so he did not notice.

"Lettuce," said Ben Isaac. "Good lettuce."

"I guess lettuce is all right too," said Ida, who hated lettuce.

"Better than all right. There is something great about lettuce."

"Yes?" said Ida in a tone that tried, unsuccessfully, to hide the question mark.

"Yes," said Ben Isaac Goldman forcefully. "And what is great about lettuce is that it is not hamburger." He laughed.

"Or ice cream," said Ida, and laughed with him, and their strides lengthened as they searched more diligently for a restaurant that served good vegetables. And lettuce.

So this at last was the promised land, Ben Isaac Goldman thought. What life was all about. A job, a place to live, a woman on his arm. The meaning of life. Not revenge. Not destruction. Here, there was no one checking on him, no meetings, no bugged telephones, no dust, no soldiers, no sand, no desert, no war.

He talked all through dinner at a little place with wrinkled peas, white carrots that grew soggy, and lettuce no crisper than wet blotting paper.

By the time their coffee came, weak and bitter as it was, Ben was holding Ida's hands in his on the table.

"America is truly a golden country," he said.

Ida Bernard nodded, watching Ben's broad, jolly face, a face she had seen every day going to work at the hamburger palace, and that she had finally conspired to meet at the glove-disposal unit in the parking lot.

She realized she had never seen Goldman smile until now. She had never seen the twinkle in his deep brown eyes or color in his pale cheeks until now.

"They think I am a dull old man," Goldman said, waving his arm to sweep together every frizz-haired hamburger jockey in the country who resented assistant managers who told them not to pick their noses near the food. Goldman's swinging arm bumped against a newspaper tucked precariously into the pocket of a man's raincoat hanging on the coatrack. It fell to the floor, and Goldman, looking around embarrassedly, bent to pick it up. As he leaned over, he kept talking.

"Aaah, what do they know?" he said. "Children. They have not . . ." His voice trailed off as his eyes fixed on a corner of the newspaper.

"Yes?" said Ida Bernard. "They have not what?"

"Seen what I have seen," said Goldman. His face had gone ash white. He clutched the paper in his hand as if it were a baton and he were a world-class relay runner.

"I must go now," he said. "Thank you for a nice evening."

Then, still clutching the paper, he stumbled up out of his seat and left, without looking back.

The waiter tiredly asked Ida if that would be all. He did not seem surprised at Goldman's sudden departure. The restaurant's culinary arts often had that effect on the digestion of senior citizens, people old enough to remember when things had been better.

Ida nodded and paid the check, but as she got up to leave, she noted Goldman's hat on the coat rack. He was not to be seen on the street outside, but on the inside band of his hat, his name and address had been printed twice in indelible ink.

5

His address was only a few blocks from where she stood, so she walked.

She passed the devastated blocks of business, their doors chained and their windows fenced in against the human storm of Baltimore. She passed the open doors and boarded windows of a dozen bars. The Flamingo Club and the Pleze Walk Inn. She passed a block of squat four-family houses, each with the same design, the same television aerials, and the same fat old mommas out on the stoops in their rocking chairs, fanning the soot away from their faces.

Goldman lived in an apartment building that was, to Ida's eyes, a forbidding brick square, chipped and worn, like a stone castle that had been under attack by the Huns for the past two hundred years. The street on which he lived had survived the murderous race riots of ten years ago, only to die, instead, of natural causes.

Ida felt another twinge of pity for the little man. The maternal instincts that had lain dormant since the death of her husband, her dear Nathan, rose up like a desert wind. She would sweep away Goldman's past and give them both something to live for. Then she would cook for him, clean for him, remind him to wear his rubbers on wet days, buy him new white gloves every day, and never serve hamburgers or ice cream.

Ida found the barely discernible "Goldman" inked under a button inside the front door, and pushed it. After thirty seconds of silence, she pushed the button again. Could he have gone somewhere else? She pictured him wandering the city, being attacked by roving groups of winos and junkies.

The intercom crackled. A small voice said, "Go away."

Ida leaned up close to the intercom and shouted: "Ben, it's Ida. I have your hat."

Silence.

"Ben? Really. There's nothing to be afraid of. It's me. Ida."

Silence.

"Please, Ben. I just want to give you your hat."

A few seconds later, there was a piercing buzz that nearly separated Ida from her stockings. The door popped open, and Ida quickly went inside.

The hallway smelled of urine, vomit, and age, which had scored a knockout victory over a heavy layer of Lysol. The stairs were concrete with a metal bannister. A naked forty-watt bulb illuminated each landing.

As she climbed each flight of stairs, the sounds of Pennsylvania Avenue assailed her, the honking of the white seven-year-old Cadillacs, the screeches of black kids and hookers.

She found Apartment A-412 in the corner. Ida stood on the cold floor under the loose, gray acoustical tile ceiling for a moment, then knocked.

The door opened immediately, to her surprise, and Goldman, who seemed to have aged in an hour, gestured quickly and said, "Hurry, come in, hurry."

Inside, the street sounds were dimmed by the sheer weight of plaster. The only light was from

7

a bathroom bulb, but that was enough to let Ida see the environment Ben Isaac lived in.

As she took in the dirty beige walls, the worn green carpet, and the one broken-down brown chair, she thought the place was enough to give anyone nightmares. Her mental redecorating stopped as Ben Isaac came before her.

His eyes were haunted and his hands were shaking. His shirt was untucked and his belt was undone.

"You have my hat?" he said, grabbing at it. "Good. Now you must go. Hurry!"

He tried to move her out without touching her, as if contact would mean instant contamination, but Ida dodged nimbly and moved for the light switch.

"Please, Ben. I won't hurt you," she said as she flicked the switch. Goldman blinked in the stark one hundred and fifty watts.

"You must not be afraid of me. I would hate that," Ida said.

She moved toward the bathroom to switch off that light. She saw the wall and the seat of the toilet covered by wetness. The tile wall was imprinted with oily fingerprints, and the towel racks were empty so that they created a makeshift arm rest.

Ida ignored it only with an effort and switched off the bathroom light. Her care was tinged with pity as she turned back to Goldman, who looked ready to cry.

She looked into his eyes and opened her arms.

"You must not be ashamed, Ben. I understand. Your past can't hurt you." She smiled, even though she didn't completely understand and she had no idea what his past was.

Goldman's wide face was completely white, and he stood unsteadily. He stared into Ida's open, friendly, dream-filled eyes, then collapsed onto the bed in tears.

Ida came over to the old man and sat next to him. She touched his shoulder and asked, "What is it, Ben?"

Goldman continued to cry and waved his hand at the door. Ida looked but saw only a crumbled newspaper. "You want me to leave?" she said.

Ben Isaac was suddenly up and moving. He hung up his hat, picked up the newspaper, gave it to Ida, then went over to the kitchen sink and started to wash his hands. It was the newspaper he had picked up in the restaurant.

Ida glanced at the headline, which read, "SEX ROMPS THROUGH TREASURY DEPT.," then turned back to Goldman.

"What is it, Ben?" she repeated.

Goldman left the water running while he pointed to an item in the lower righthand corner. Then he went back to washing his hands.

Ida read as a soapy drop of water began to soak through the news item:

MUTILATED BODY FOUND IN NEGEV, Tel Aviv, Israel (AP)—A mutilated corpse was found early this morning on an excavation site by a group of young archeologists. The remains were originally described as being in the shape of a swastika, the Nazi symbol of power in Germany over three decades ago.

Since then, Israeli officials have negated that report and identified the remains as those of

9

Ephraim Boris Hegez, an industrialist in Jerusalem.

When asked about the murder, Tochala Delit, a government spokesman, stated that the remains were probably left after an Arab terrorist attack. Delit said that he doubts that the excavations for evidence of Israel's two original temples, dating as early as 586 B.C. will be interrupted in any way by the grisly discovery.

The Israeli authorities have no comment as to the motive or murderer and no suspects have been named.

Ida Bernard stopped reading and looked up. Ben Isaac Goldman was drying his hands over and over with a used Handi-wipe.

"Ben . . . ," she began.

"I know who killed that man," said Goldman, "and I know why. They killed him because he ran away. Ida, I come from Israel. I ran away too."

Goldman dropped the paper towel on the floor and sat next to Ida on the bed, head in his hands.

"You do?" she said. "Then you must call the police at once!"

"I can't," Goldman said. "They will find me and kill me too. What they are planning to do is so terrible that even I could not face it. Not after all these years . . ."

"Then call the newspapers," Ida insisted. "No one can trace you through them. Look."

Ida picked up the newspaper from her lap.

"It's the *Washington Post*. Call them up and tell them you have a big story. They'll listen to you."

Goldman grabbed her hands fiercely, giving Ida an electric thrill.

"You think so? There is a chance? They can end this nightmare?"

"Of course," Ida said kindly. "I know you can do it, Ben. I trust you." Ida Goldman. Not a bad name. It had a nice ring to it.

Ben Isaac stared in awe. He had dreams of his own. But could it be? Could this handsome woman have the answer? Goldman fumbled for the phone that lay near the foot of the bed and dialed Information.

"Hello? Information? Do you have the number of the *Washington Post* newspaper?"

Ida beamed.

"Oh? What?" Goldman put his hand over the receiver. "Administrative offices or subscription?" he asked.

"Administrative," Ida replied.

"Administrative," said Goldman. "Yes? Yes, two, two, three ... six, zero, zero, zero. Thank you." Goldman hung up, glanced in Ida's direction, then dialed again.

"Two, two, three ... ," his finger moved, "six, zero, zero."

"Ask for Redford or Hoffm ... , I mean Woodward and Bernstein," said Ida.

"Oh, yes," said Goldman, "Hello? May I speak to ... Redwood or Hoffstein, please?"

Ida smiled in spite of herself.

"Oh?" said Goldman. "What? Yes, of course. Thank you." He turned to Ida. "They're switching me to a reporter," he said, and waited, sweating. "Ida, do you really think they can help me?"

Ida nodded. Goldman gathered strength from her.

"Ida, I have to tell you the truth now. I've, I've watched you before. I have thought to myself, what a handsome woman. Could a woman like this come to like me? I hardly dared hope, Ida. But I could do nothing because I was waiting for my past to find me out. Many years ago I promised to do something. What I did back then was necessary. It was and had to be. But what they are planning to do is mindless. Total destruction."

Goldman paused, looking deep into Ida's eyes. She held her breath, biting her lower lip, giving her the look of a love-sick teenager. She wasn't even listening to his confession. She knew what she wanted to hear and was only waiting for that.

"I am an old man," Goldman began, "but when I was young I was ... Hello?" Goldman directed his attention back to the phone. He had been connected.

"Hello, Redman? No, no, I'm sorry. Yes. Uh, well ... ," Goldman put his hand over the receiver again. "What should I say?" he asked Ida.

"I have a big story for you," said Ida.

"I have a big story for you," said Goldman into the phone.

"About the dead businessman in the Israeli desert," said Ida.

"About the dead businessman in the Israeli desert," said Goldman. "Yes? What?" Goldman nodded excitedly at Ida, putting his hand over the receiver again. "They want to talk to me," he reported.

Ida nodded excitedly back. Finally, she thought, I have found him. Goldman is a good man. She would get him out of his trouble—what could he have done that was so bad?—and then they could keep each other company through their old age. At last, something, someone to live for again. The hell of Baltimore wouldn't matter. All those snotty youngsters wouldn't matter. Medicare, Social Security, and pensions wouldn't matter. They would have each other.

"No," Goldman was saying, "no, you must come here. Yes, right away. My name is Ben Isaac Goldman, apartment A dash four-twelve," and he gave the address on Pennsylvania Avenue. "Yes, right away."

He hung up. Sweat clung to his face, but he was smiling.

"How did I do?" he asked.

Ida leaned over and hugged him. "Fine," she said, "I'm sure you have done the right thing." He clung to her. "I'm sure you've done the right thing," she repeated.

Goldman leaned back. "You are a fine woman, Ida. The kind they do not make anymore. I am proud to be with you. I am old and tired, but you make me feel strong."

"You are strong," said Ida Bernard.

"Maybe you are right," Goldman smiled wearily, "maybe things can be good again."

Ida put her hand on his wet brow and began to wipe the sweat away. "We will have each other," she said.

Goldman looked at her with a new, dawning awareness. She looked back with tenderness.

"We'll have each other," he repeated.

The loneliness and pain of fifty collected years flooded out of them and they collapsed into each other's arms.

There was a knock on the door.

Their heads snapped up, one in shock, the other in disappointment. Goldman looked at Ida, who shrugged diffidently, beginning to pat her hair back in place.

"The *Post* probably has a nearby Baltimore office," she said.

Secured by her presence, Goldman nodded and then opened the door.

A hard-looking man of medium height stood outside in a simple, but expensive suit. Goldman blinked, taking in the hard face and the dark wavy hair. Goldman looked for a press card or a pad and pencil, but saw only empty hands and thick wrists.

But when the man smiled and spoke, Goldman lost his strength of a moment before and stumbled back.

"Heil Hitler," the man said and pushed open the door.

Goldman soiled his pants.

Dustin Woodman pressed all the call buttons in the foyer of the apartment building on Pennsylvania Avenue and cursed.

He cursed his parents for not naming him Maurice or Chauncey, or Ignatz. He cursed Warner Brothers for putting up $8 million for a certain movie and cursed the public for making that certain movie a smash hit. He cursed the switchboard girl for thinking it funny to connect every crackpot, weirdo, joker, housewife, or wino who called in for Woodward, Bernstein, Hoffman, or Redford.

And he also had a gold-plated, solid platinum

curse for the editor who made him answer all these calls. "In the paper's interest," he had been told. Up the paper's ass, he thought.

He got them all, every call to the main office by every dippo who had congressmen dancing naked in his refrigerator or who had uncovered a conspiracy to poison feminine hygiene sprays. Woodman got them all.

The door buzzed and clicked open. Woodman pushed on it while reaching into his pocket for a stick of sugarless gum, recommended by four out of five dentists for patients who care about their teeth. Woodman was beginning to develop the second of the newspaperman's three curses, a flaccid spare tire, broadening his waist. He had always had the first curse—no suntan—and he was too young yet for the third curse—alcoholism—but he could do something about the second, so he cut out sugar and began to take stairs two at a time for exercise.

The door buzzed again.

Woodman took the stairs two at a time until he discovered that hopping up stairs and chewing gum at the same time was a little too much exercise.

He scratched his earthy blond hair as he rounded the third-floor landing. He felt wetness bounce off his middle finger and slide onto his hair.

What a place, he thought, stopping. Complete with leaky water pipes.

Below him, he heard the door buzz again as he brought his hand down and shook off the moisture.

The floor and his trouser leg were suddenly

dotted with red. Woodman brought his hand up and looked at it. Swirled around his middle finger, like the tattoo of a lightning bolt, was a streak of blood.

He looked up and saw a small trickle of blood dripping over from the fourth-floor landing. Woodman sucked in his breath and grabbed his pencil, although he did not know why. He held it in his right hand as he went up the stairs cautiously. In his mind, he was composing leads for his story.

"The stink of blood emanated from a peaceful-looking Baltimore flat . . ."

He rejected that.

He reached the fourth-floor landing. He saw that the red stream was coming from the slightly opened door marked A-412. His mind dictated to him: "Acting on a hunch, this reporter fought fear to discover . . ."

He pushed the door open and stopped.

Inside the room were two gory swastikas made from human limbs. One was shorter, hairier than the other, but both fit within the huge pond of blood. But Woodman didn't see that. All he saw was a huge scoop of red. A Book-of-the-Month-Club nonfiction selection or, at least, a Literary Guild novelization heralding his addition to *The New York Times* Best Seller List.

That was just the beginning. When Woodman looked in the bathroom and saw the two heads lying together in the bathtub, he really saw the movie, starring Clint Eastwood as him. He saw Merv Griffin and Johnny Carson and Book Beat on PBS and the NBC-TV special production.

Woodman stood, taking notes furiously. He had

no idea that his paper and the paperback publishers would want nothing to do with just another grisly murder. They wanted conspiracy. They wanted something spectacular.

Woodman's item was buried on page thirty-two of the next day's edition, and he went back to chasing dancing congressmen and poisoned feminine sprays. It was Wednesday before his reporting came to the attention of Dr. Harold W. Smith of Rye, New York.

And to him the piece of news meant more than any *Playboy* serialization or *Reader's Digest* condensation. It meant that there might be no more Middle East soon.

17

CHAPTER TWO

His name was Remo, and the tiny flakes of rust built up under his fingernails like grains of salt. They were not so much dangerous as annoying, and he could hear the packed metal chips click against the steel structure as his fingers kept going higher and higher above his head as if cutting a path in space for his body to follow.

The body moved without thought and slowly, like a metronome that might not make another click. The breath came deep, holding all the oxygen for another count. The legs were relaxed, but always moving, not really fighting gravity by upward thrust, but ignoring gravity, moving in a time and space of their own.

The fingertips reached farther overhead, the packed rust touched the metal with a clicking sound, and the legs followed, and the arms stretched again.

Remo felt the chill of the height and took his

body temperature down to meet it. Down below, Paris looked like a great gray tangle of blocks and black wires.

His arms stretched again over his head, and his fingertips felt the damp top of a horizontal metal bar, and even more slowly, he brought the rest of his body up to the level of the railing, because trying to hurry the last few steps would destroy his unity with the surface, like a skier who makes a great run down a slope and then tries to hurry into the ski lodge to brag about it, falls on the steps, and breaks an arm. Slow was the secret.

Then Remo's body was up and over the metal bar. He stood on a platform and looked down the sloping sides of the Eiffel Tower at Paris below him.

"No one told me this tower was rusty," he said. "But you people put cheese in your potatoes. How can you expect anybody who puts cheese in potatoes to keep a tower unrusted?"

Remo's companion assured the thin, thick-waisted American that that was true. Absolutely true. Definitely, naturally, *certainement!*

The Frenchman knew that Remo was thick-wristed, because that was about all he could see from where he hung, suspended over Paris.

When Remo did not respond, the man gave him a few more "definitelys," his carefully groomed Vandyke beard bobbing up and down.

"Do you know I haven't had a potato in over ten years?" Remo said. "But when I did have them, I didn't put cheese in them."

"Only Americans know how to eat," the Frenchman said. Remo's thin body moved into his view as the wind whirled about, and the Frenchman's dangling body twisted, and Remo's thick wrist lay across the vision of his right eye as Remo's hand was wrapped around his neck.

Remo nodded. "Steak," said Remo. "Remember steak?"

The Frenchman on the end of Remo's arm hurriedly reported that he himself could personally take Remo to at least a dozen, make that two dozen, places where he would buy Remo the nicest, fattest, juiciest steak he had ever had. Two steaks, a half-dozen steaks, a herd of steer. A ranch.

"I don't eat steak anymore either," Remo said.

"Whatever you like, I will get for you," the Frenchman said. "We can go now. Anywhere you like. We will take my jet. Just put me on the tower. You do not even have to bring me over the railing. Just put me near a rail. I will climb down myself. I saw how easily you climbed up."

The Frenchman swallowed heavily and tried to smile. He looked like a hairy grapefruit being slit open.

"Down is even easier than up," Remo said. "Try it."

He opened his hand and the Frenchman dropped five feet onto a metal crossbar. He tried clasping himself around it, but his hands, which had never done anything more strenuous than lift a rum cooler, would not grip. He felt the wet flakes of rust break loose from the metal and slide away underneath him. His arms, which he himself had never used to lift any of the thousands of kilos of heroin and cocaine he exported each year, did not have the strength to hang on.

21

His legs, which were used only to walk from car to building and back to car, did not work right.

The Frenchman's limbs slid across the metal, desperately searching for an easy grip, but he felt himself sliding down and across. He felt cold air encircle his legs as they slipped loose and swung out over the city. His mouth opened, and the night was filled with a squealing, bleating noise as if a pig had collided with a sheep at sixty miles an hour.

Suddenly the hand of the American was back under his chin and his body once again hung three feet away from the Eiffel Tower.

"You see?" said Remo. "If it wasn't for me, you would have fallen. And I don't want that to happen. I want to drop you myself."

The Frenchman's color left his face and slid down to fill the front of his pants.

"Oh, hohohohoho," he managed, trying not to move. "Always joking, you Americans, yes?"

"No," said Remo. He had finished cleaning the rust from the fingernails of his left hand and now he transferred the Frenchman to that hand while he cleaned the nails of his right hand.

"Ah, you Americans. Always playing so hard to get. I remember. Once, your playful ones slammed my fingers in the top drawer of a desk. But when I gave them something ... I will give you something. A piece of the drug action, you leave me alone, no? How much do you want? Half? All?"

Remo shook his head and started climbing again.

The Frenchman babbled about how he had always been a good friend of America's. Remo didn't hear him because his mind was on becoming one with the red, flaking iron as his two legs and one arm bent, then straightened, bent then straightened, bent then straightened.

He tried to avoid thinking of how no one had told him the tower was rusty. He avoided thinking about how simple this project had been. His assignment had been to discourage the drug trade throughout France. But the U.S. government could name no clear-cut criminals, only very likely suspects. Which meant that the Treasury Department and the Drug Abuse Administration and at least a dozen other agencies would be wound all around themselves and each other, trying to uncover incriminating evidence. And, of course, the CIA was no longer any good overseas because it was still busy making sure its fly wasn't open at home.

So the job filtered down to one very special agent, Remo, who bypassed all the complications with a simple brand of interrogation.

Talk or die. Simple. Worked every time. And so he had found the kingpin, the Frenchman with the Vandyke.

The Frenchman was talking about how France was helped by America in World War I, after France had collapsed upon the firing of the first bullet.

As Remo reached the second tourist level of the closed-for-the-night tower, the French connection on the end of his arm recalled with brilliant clarity how America helped France in World War II when the silly French bastards sat behind the Maginot Line playing bezique while

Hitler's forces first outflanked, then overwhelmed, them.

Even as Remo got halfway up the third level and the going sloped measurably steeper, the Frenchman declared his support of America in its battle over world oil prices.

"France is a good friend of America," the man declared while trying to get his fingers into Remo's eyes. "I like many Americans, Spiro Agnew, John Connally, Frank Sinatra . . ."

Remo looked out over Paris as he came to rest on the sloping arch just above the third sightseeing level, nine hundred and fifty feet above sea level.

It was a clear night, brightly lit by the homes, outdoor cafés, theaters, discos, and business offices in France's capital. Every light in the city seemed to be on. No energy crises here, no sir, not with their hands in every pocket and their heads kissing every ass in sight.

The drug merchant started to sing Yankee Doodle. Remo waited until he got to "stuck ze fezzer in ze hat," then dropped him.

The man hit before he got a chance to call himself macaroni.

There was a splatting thud that caused night strollers to look up at the tower. All they saw was a man who looked a little like a night watchman standing on the second level looking up as well. After a few seconds, the night watchman continued on his way and the pedestrians paid attention to the squished body in the street.

The "night watchman" skipped down the remaining stairs, whistling "Frère Jacques." He waited, then hopped over the eight and a half foot wrought iron fence and headed back into town.

Remo trotted through the early morning crowds of French teenagers trying to be American at their "le discos" and "le hamburger joints" and in their "le blue jeans" and "le chinos."

Remo was American, and he didn't see what the big deal was. When he was their age, he was not dancing till dawn, eating "le quarter-pounder avec fromage"; he was Remo Williams, pounding a beat as a rookie patrolman in Newark, New Jersey, and dancing with the corrupt administration to keep alive.

And his honest idealism got him a bum murder rap, and a one-way ticket to the electric chair.

Except the electric chair hadn't worked.

Remo wound his way through narrow streets until he found a side entrance to the Paris Hilton. He peeled off his night watchman clothes and dropped them into the garbage can, then brushed the wrinkles from his casual blue slacks and black T-shirt, which he had worn underneath the uniform.

And that was life and death. A borrowed night watchman's uniform, a climb up the outside of a tower the French were too lazy to keep unrusted, a public execution of a drug dealer to serve as discouragement for anyone planning to step into his suddenly empty shoes, and brush wrinkles from your blue slacks and black T-shirt. Ho hum.

Remo's "death" in the electric chair had been more exciting. His death had been faked so he could join a super-secret organization. It seemed that all was not well in the United States. One had only to stick one's head out the window, and

25

if one still had one's head when he pulled it back inside, one could see. Crime was threatening to take over the country.

So a young president created an organization that didn't exist, an organization called CURE, and it drafted a dead man who no longer existed, Remo Williams, to work outside the Constitution to protect the Constitution.

Its first and only director was Dr. Harold W. Smith and as far as Remo was concerned, he barely existed either. Rational, logical, analytical, unimaginative, Smith lived in a world where two plus two always equaled four, even in a world where children were taught every day on the six o'clock news that tastelessness plus brass equaled stardom.

Remo strolled through the Paris Hilton lobby, which was filled with smiling, mustachioed bellboys in berets, busy practicing their professional indifference.

Except for them, the lobby was empty and no one paid the dark-haired American any mind as he walked to "le stairs," and trotted up to "le neuf floor," past "le coffee shop," "le drug store," "le soufflé restaurant," "le bistro" snack shop, and "l'ascot" clothing store.

Remo reached "le neuf floor" suite in a couple of seconds and found Chiun where he had left him, sitting on a grass mat in the middle of the living room floor.

To a stranger entering the room, Chiun would appear to be an aged Oriental, small and frail, with white tufts of hair fluttering out from the sides of his otherwise bald head. This was correct

26

as far as it went, which was approximately as far as saying that a tree is green.

For Chiun was also the Master of Sinanju, the latest in a centuries-long line of Korean Master assassins, and he had taught Remo the art of Sinanju.

From Sinanju had come all the other martial arts—karate, kung fu, aikido, tae kwan do—and each resembled it only as a cut of beef resembled the whole steer. Some disciplines were filet mignon and some were sirloin steak and some were chopped chuck. But Sinanju was the whole steer.

Chiun had taught Remo to catch bullets, kill taxis, climb rusty towers, all with the power of his mind and the limitless resources of his body, and Remo was not sure if he would ever forgive him for it.

At first, it had been easy. The president of the United States would tap Smith on the shoulder, and Smith would point and say "kill," and Remo would rip up whatever Chiun was pointing at.

At first, it had been fun. But then one assignment led to another, then another, then dozens more, and he found he no longer remembered the faces of the dead. And as his spirit changed, his body changed. He could no longer eat like the rest of humankind, nor sleep, nor love. Chiun's training was too complete, too effective, and Remo became something more than human, but something less than human too, lacking the great human seasoning of imperfection.

Alone, Remo could wipe out a given army at a given time. Together, he and Chiun could give the bowels of the earth diarrhea.

But right now, the Master was giving Remo a headache.

"Remo," he said in his high-pitched voice that encompassed all misery, "is that you?"

Remo walked across the room toward the bathroom. Chiun knew damn well it was him and probably had known it was him even before he made it to the seventh floor. But he talked quickly because he recognized the tone in Chiun's voice.

It was his "pity-this-poor-old-crapped-upon-Korean-who-must-bear-the-weight-of-the-world-on-his-frail-shoulders-without-the-help-of-his-ungrateful-American-ward" voice.

"Yes, it is I, America's premiere assassin, with powers and abilities far beyond those of mortal men. Remo! Who can change the course of corrupt government, bend lawyers in his bare hands."

Remo made it into the bathroom, still talking.

"Faster than the SST, more powerful than the Olympics, able to leap the continents in a single bound . . ." Remo turned on the water, hoping he could drown out Chiun's voice. But the voice, when it came, came just loud enough to be heard over the rush of water.

"Who will help a poor old man get some much-needed peace? When will these injustices end?"

Remo turned on both faucets. He could still hear Chiun. So he turned on the shower.

"I do not like this new work," came Chiun's voice as if he were standing inside Remo's head and talking out. Remo flushed the toilet.

The world had changed since Chiun had originally trained Remo. CURE had seen to that. You could not keep arranging astronomical amounts of corruption convictions, keep thinning out the roles of organized crime, and keep solving the everyday crises of a country with the military strength to wipe out the world one hundred times over without attracting attention.

So now, all over the world, hands were being tentatively reached out to clasp those of the United States. Some were barbed, some were weak, some were strong.

The Constitution became more than a pact with America's people, it had become a promise to other countries. Remo's job now was to protect that promise—a job that had formerly been done by other agencies. CURE was taking care of the whole earth now.

Naturally, Congress disemboweling the CIA had nothing to do with CURE's new assignments. They would be the first to tell you that.

"I miss my daytime dramas," finished Chiun's voice, as if he had been shouting into an empty auditorium.

Remo knew he could never win, so he turned off the shower, washed his hands in the sink, turned off the faucets, and came back into the living room.

"What do you mean?" he asked, drying his hands on a towel emblazoned with the huge green letters, PARIS HILTON. "Never mind, I know. Smith stopped sending you your video tapes."

Chiun remained sitting in the lotus position, his head turned slightly to the side, his eyes cocked and ready to fire.

29

"I could understand dishonesty. It is a characteristic of you whites. But deceit? What is the use of a lifetime of dedication?"

Remo moved over to Chiun's personal video playback machine, which was lying on its side on the other side of the room.

"Get with it, Chiun. What's the matter?" Remo asked, picking up the machine and bringing it over.

"Observe," said Chiun, as he snapped a videotape cassette up and into the playback slot.

Remo watched as 525 gray vertical lines spread across the screen, coming together into a color moving picture of a housewife in a childish minidress carrying a large bowl into a living room.

The housewife wore her long brown hair in two fat braids with bangs above her wide oval eyes and overbite below.

"I brought some chicken soup for him," the housewife said to another housewife actress who looked like a chicken in slacks. "I heard he was sick."

The chicken housewife took the bowl and gave it to her bundled-up, drunk husband, then the two women sat on a couch, to talk.

Remo was about to ask what was wrong with this, since it looked as slow and dull as any other soap opera Chiun felt the need to watch, when the TV husband fell forward in a drunken stupor and drowned in the bowl of chicken soup.

Remo stared as Chiun sputtered: "Emperor Smith promised to send me my daytime dramas. The glorious 'As the Planet Revolves.' The golden 'All My Offspring.' Instead I receive . . . ,"

30

Chiun raised his already high voice to a squeal, " 'Mary Hartman, Mary Hartman!' "

Remo smirked as the ladies discovered the smothered man on the screen. "I don't see what is so awful, Little Father."

"Of course, you wouldn't, pale piece of pig's ear. Any garbage would look good to a man who turns on all the water outlets to drown out his mentor's proclamations."

Remo turned to the Korean. "What's wrong with it?" he asked, motioning to the set.

"What is wrong?" exclaimed Chiun, as if any child could see. "Where is the drunken doctor? Where is the unwed mother, the suicidal wife? Where are the children on drugs? Where are all the things that have made America great?"

Remo glanced back at the video screen. "I'm sure they're there, Chiun, just handled with a little more realism, that's all."

"You whites find a way to ruin everything, don't you?" said Chiun. "If I want realism, I talk to you or some other imbecile. If I want beauty, I watch my daytime dramas."

Chiun rose from his mat in a smooth movement that gave the impression of pale yellow smoke rising. He moved to four blue and gold lacquered steamer trunks that lay in the corner atop and crowding out one of the suite's beds. As Remo watched more of the TV show, Chiun opened the trunk and started hurling out merchandise.

Remo turned as small bars of soap started dropping around him.

"What are you doing?" he inquired, removing

31

a washcloth with a Holiday Inn imprint from his shoulder.

"I am trying to find the contract between the House of Sinanju and Emperor Smith. I am sure that sending 'Mary Hartman, Mary Hartman' instead of 'The Old and the Agitated' is a breach of our agreement. If this is how they value my services, I am leaving before the worst comes."

Remo went over to where Chiun's small frame had disappeared into the large trunk.

"Hold on, Little Father. It's just a mistake. They haven't done anything else wrong, have they?"

Chiun rose quickly, a feigned look of surprise on his wrinkled parchment face.

"They sent me you, didn't they?" he cackled, then sank into the luggage again. "Heh, heh, heh," his voice echoed. "They sent me you, didn't they? Heh, heh, heh."

Remo began to pick up the trunk's contents that littered the suite floor like autumn leaves after a rainstorm.

"Hold it, hold it. What's this, Little Father?" Remo held a small bottle up to the light. "Seagram's, courtesy of American Airlines?" He picked up another. "Johnny Walker Black, Fly me, Eastern Airlines? Smirnoff's, thanks for flying TWA?"

Chiun rose again from the trunk, a slow-blooming flower of innocence.

"One never knows when those things might be needed," he said.

"We don't drink. And what's this?" continued Remo, stooping to pick up more items from the floor, "Matches from the Showboat, The Four

32

Seasons Restaurant, Howard Johnson's? Toothpicks? These mints must be five years old."

"They were offered to me," said Chiun. "It would be bad manners not to accept."

Remo held up a final item.

"An ashtray with Cinzano on it?"

Chiun leaned over, looking slightly perplexed. "I do not remember that. Is it yours? Have you been smuggling junk in with my treasures?"

Remo turned back to the TV screen. "I've always wondered what you filled those trunks with. I've been lugging a junk shop with me all these years."

"I cannot find the contract," declared Chiun, "so I find myself unable to quit. Because to me, unlike you and that madman Smith, my word of honor is sacred."

"Awwww," Remo clucked in sympathy.

"However, I must take steps to bring these annoyances to an end. Smith must increase the payment to the village of Sinanju and send real tapes from real shows."

"Come on, Little Father, Sinanju must be getting enough from us by now to platinum-plate your outhouses."

"Gold, not platinum," said Chiun. "They only deliver gold. And it is not enough. It is never enough. Do you not remember the terrible devastation that gripped our tiny village just a scant few years ago?"

"It's enough. And that was at least a thousand years ago," said Remo, knowing his protest was not enough to keep Chiun from his umpteenth retelling of the legend of Sinanju, a poor fishing village in North Korea that was forced to hire its people out as master assassins to avoid drowning their children in the bay because of poverty.

And for centuries after, the Masters of Sinanju had done admirably. At least in the monetary sense. Chiun, the present Master was doing the best of all. Even allowing for inflation.

"So you see," finished Chiun, "how enough is never enough, and the seas and sky never change, yet Sinanju stays the same."

Remo tried to stifle a yawn, purposely failed, then said, "Fine. Good. Can I go to sleep now? Smitty is supposed to contact us soon. I need my rest."

"Yes, my son. You can go to sleep. Just as soon as we have taken steps to protect others from this Mary Hartman, Mary Hartman."

"We?" Remo said from the bed. "Why we?"

"I need you," said Chiun, "because there is some stupid trivial menial work involved." Chiun moved over to the desk, opened the top drawer, and pulled out a piece of paper and pen. "I want to know who is responsible for 'Mary Hartman, Mary Hartman,'" he said.

"I think it's Norman Lear, Norman Lear," said Remo.

Chiun nodded. "I have heard of this man. He has done much to ruin American television." The Master lifted the pen and paper and dropped them onto Remo's stomach. "Take a letter."

Remo grumbled, watching Chiun move to his mat and settle softly into the lotus position. "Are you ready?" the Master inquired.

"Yeah, yeah," said Remo.

Chiun closed his eyes and gently positioned the backs of his hands upon his knees.

34

"Dear Norman Lear, Norman Lear," he said. "Watch out. Sign it Chiun."

Remo waited. "No sincerely or anything?" he finally asked.

"I will read it tomorrow for accuracy and then you will send it," said Chiun before he slipped into a shallow level of sleep, sitting erect upon his grass mat.

The phone was ringing, and Remo had to know whether it was for him. There were many phones ringing during the night. You could hear them through the walls. You could hear people talk and air conditioners hum, and a mouse that made it through the walls, running desperately through the building's innards. It was pursued by nothing, because there was no other sound moving with it.

There were sounds in the night; it was never quiet. For Remo, it had not been quiet for more than a decade. The meat eaters and the warriors slept with their brains blanketed, but it wasn't sleep. It was unconsciousness. Real sleep, that cool rest of mind and body, floated gently, aware of what was around it. You could no more turn off your mind than you could your breath. And why should you?

Primitive man probably didn't. How could he and live to create modern man? Most people slept like meatloaves. But as Chiun had taught him, to sleep like that was to make oneself dead before one's time, so Remo heard everything as he slept. Like listening to a concert next door. He was aware of it, but not part of it. Then the

35

phone rang. And since he realized it was too loud to be next door, he got up and answered it.

As he lifted the receiver off the hook, he heard Chiun mumble, "Must you let that thing ring for hours before you bestir yourself?"

"Stuff it, Little Father," Remo said. "Hello," he growled at the phone.

"I'm here," said a voice so acerb Remo's ear felt as if it were puckering up.

"Congratulations, Smitty. You've made my night."

Dr. Harold W. Smith sounded disappointed. "I thought by contacting you this early I would avoid the sarcasm."

"The CURE sarcasm service is open twenty-four hours a day. Call again this time tomorrow and see."

"Enough," Smith said. "Have you fixed that faulty French connection?"

"Is the Fonz cool?"

"Where is the Fonz?" asked Smith.

"Never mind," said Remo. "Job's done."

"Good. I have another assignment for you."

"What now?" asked Remo. "Don't I ever get any sleep? Who've we got to zap this time?"

"Not over the phone," Smith said. "The outdoor café on the north side of the hotel. In twenty minutes."

There was a click, then a dial tone that Remo swore sounded as if it had a French accent.

"That was that lunatic Smith," Chiun said, still immobile in the lotus position on the mat.

"Who else at this hour?"

"Good. He and I must talk."

36

"If you wanted to talk to him, why didn't you answer the telephone?"

"Because that is servant's work," Chiun said. "Did you send it?"

"Send what?"

"The message to Norman Lear, Norman Lear," Chiun said.

"Little Father, I just got up."

"I cannot trust you to do anything right. You should have sent it by now. He who waits waits forever."

"And a stitch in time saves nine, a penny saved is a penny earned, early to bed and early to rise. Which way is north?"

Harold Smith, the director of CURE, sat among the colorful, babbling young French patrons at the early-morning bistro like a cockroach at a cocktail party.

As Remo slid into a seat across the simple white table, he saw that Smith wore his customary gray suit, vest, and annoying Dartmouth tie. Countries changed, years passed, some died and some lived, but Harold W. Smith and his suit remained eternally the same.

Chiun parked himself on the next table, which was, mercifully, unoccupied, so that Chiun did not have to unoccupy it. Customers stole glances at the trio, and one young man identified Chiun as Sun Mung Moon in town for a pop rally.

The hired help had seen the trio's kind before, however. The older one in the twenty-year-old suit must be the producer. The thin one in the black T-shirt was the director, and the Oriental couldn't be a servant since he was sitting on a

37

table as if he owned the restaurant, so he must be the actor playing Charlie Chan or Fu Manchu or something. Just another silly American film company.

"Hi, Smitty," said Remo. "What's worth waking me up for?"

"Remo," said Smith, by way of greeting. "Chiun."

"Right again," said Remo.

"Hail to the Great Emperor, wise guardian of the Constitution, ageless in wisdom and generosity," said Chiun, bowing low, even with his legs crossed on the table.

Smith turned to Remo. "What does he want now? When he calls me 'Great Emperor' he wants something."

Remo shrugged. "You'll know when he tells you. What's happening?"

Smith talked for approximately twelve minutes in the annoying ring-around way he had mastered during the bug-infested sixties. Remo gathered that there had been two deaths of Israelis recently, thousands of miles apart, but they tied in to something much bigger.

"So?" he asked.

"Reports from the areas in question," said Smith, "mention a man who fits your description."

"So?" Remo repeated.

"Well," said Smith, in a way of explanation, "the victims were found mutilated."

Remo screwed his face up in disgust. "Come on, Smitty, I don't work like that. Besides I don't free-lance."

"I'm sorry. I just had to be sure," Smith said.

38

"We've found that both victims were involved in the nuclear area."

"What?"

Smith cleared his throat and tried again. "We have reason to believe that these deaths may signal an impending attack on a recent addition to the Israeli armament."

Remo waved a hand in front of his face as if shooing a fly away. "Run that by me again. This time, try English."

"These violent incidents might be directly related to the Israeli stockpile of powerful armaments that might threaten the entire world."

"I got it," Remo said, snapping his fingers. "You're talking about atomic bombs. He's talking about atomic bombs, Chiun," he called.

"Shhhhh," said Smith.

"Yes, shhh," said Chiun in a loud voice. "If the Emperor wishes to talk about atomic bombs, I alone will protect his right to do so. Go ahead, great one, and speak of atomic bombs in perfect safety."

Smith looked upward as if hoping to see an elevator from God.

"Wait a minute," Remo said. "You say they found a woman's body, too?"

"She was clean," Smith replied. "Probably just an innocent person who got in the way."

"Okay," said Remo. "Where do we go from here?"

"Israel," said Smith. "This might be a prelude to World War III, Remo. The two dead men had been involved with Israel's atomic weapons. With terrorists running wild there, who knows what might be going on? Any kind of incident could

39

blow up the Middle East. Perhaps the whole world."

Smith sounded as if he were reciting a recipe for chicken salad, but Remo managed to look concerned. Chiun looked overjoyed.

"Israel?" he chirped. "A Master has not visited Israel since the days of Herod the Wonderful."

Remo looked over. "Herod the Wonderful?"

Chiun returned his look brightly. "He was a much maligned man. He paid on time. And he kept his word, unlike some other emperors who promise things, then send other things."

Smith rose, managing with obvious difficulty to ignore Chiun's hinted complaints. "Find out what's happening and stop it," he told Remo. To Chiun, he said, "Be well, Master of Sinanju."

As he turned to go, Chiun said, "My heart is gladdened by your news, Emperor Smith. So gladdened that I will not disturb you with the grieving woe that besets your poor servant."

Smith shot a glance toward Remo. Remo stuck out his top front teeth in an imitation of Mary Hartman, Mary Hartman or of Hirohito, Hirohito.

"Oh, that," said Smith. "The man responsible has already been taken care of. Your daytime shows will be forwarded to you as soon as you settle in the Holy Land."

This time Chiun stood on the table before bowing, intoning graciousness and lifelong gratitude, and explaining that no matter what Remo recommended, he would not think of demanding increased tribute for the village of Sinanju, even if the cost of living had increased seven-tenths of one percent in the last month.

Seasonally adjusted.

CHAPTER THREE

In the hills of Galilee are the cities of Safed and Nazareth, where Israelis cultivate the land, raise turkeys, pick oranges, and happily exist in their Holy Christian cities.

In the bay of Haifa, one of the Mediterranean's busiest shipping ports is run between warehouses, metal foundries, oil refineries, fertilizer factories, textile mills, and glass plants.

In Judea is Jerusalem, clashing in style between the old city and its newer sections but united in feeling and faith.

And in Tel Aviv is an office where a small group of personnel are responsible for the security of Israel's nuclear bombs and for their detonation over Arab lands should Israel face destruction in a war against what some press elements in the United States insisted upon calling "their Arab neighbors." Until the body count of dead Israeli babies, murdered by Arab terrorists,

41

finally rose too high for even *The New York Times'* op-ed page's understanding of neighborliness.

On the door of the office was an inscription in Hebrew. It translated into English as Zeher Lahurban, "Remember the Destruction of the Temple." It masqueraded as an archeological study group, but its mission was to see that Israel was not reduced to being an archeological footnote to history.

Inside the office, a man sat with his feet on his desk, trying not to scratch the right side of his face.

Yoel Zabari had been told by his doctor not to scratch the right side of his face. The doctor told him not to, because the itch was psychosomatic, since, literally speaking, Yoel Zabari didn't have a right side of his face. Not unless one called a mass of flat, numbed tissue and plastic a face.

His right eye was gone, replaced by an unblinking glass globe, his right nostril was a hole in the middle of a sloping mound, and the right side of his mouth was a surgically perfect slit.

Someone had left an old sofa in a garbage pile on the street outside his office a year ago. As Zabari left the building and turned left, the couch blew up. A large chunk of metal and plastic ripped across his head from his right ear to the bridge of his nose. The left side of his head suffered only a bump where he fell.

Yoel Zabari survived the terrorist tactic. Twelve other people, rushing home to their families after work, did not.

The prime minister called it a vicious and ugly

attack upon innocent people. The new American representative for the U.N., caught between his heart and worldwide oil prices, called it no comment. Libya called it a courageous blow for the integrity of the Arab people. Uganda said it was retribution for aggression.

Zabari forced his rising hand to avoid his face and to settle onto the brown and gray curls atop his head. He was scratching his scalp when Tochala Delit, his first deputy, came in with his daily report.

"Toe," Zabari cried. "Good to see you back. How was your vacation?"

"Fine, sir," said Delit, smiling. "You are looking well yourself."

"If you say so," replied the director of the Zeher Lahurban, controller of nuclear security as well as of its archeology cover. "I have just managed to bring myself to look into the mirror again. I feel fine, but seeing only half a blush is always disconcerting."

Delit laughed without self-consciousness and sat in a plush red chair to the side of the broad green metal desk as he always did.

"The family well?" he inquired.

"As always, wonderful and the only reason for my life," Zabari said. "The light never dims in my wife's eyes, and my youngest this week wants to be a dancer. A ballerina yet." He shrugged. "That's this week. Wait till next."

Both the terror-scarred face and the gentle voice were sides of the man that was Yoel Zabari. A soldier, a spy, a war hero, an accomplished killer, and a fierce Zionist, he was also a fine husband, a good father, and a public-spirited man. His outward lack of full lips did nothing to mar his ability to communicate.

"You really should take a wife, Toe. As the Talmud says, 'An unmarried Jew is not considered a whole human being.'"

"The Talmud also says, 'The ignoramus jumps first,'" Delit replied.

Zabari laughed. "So now. What terrible news do you have for me today?"

Delit flipped open the folder on his lap.

"Our overseas agents report that two more American spies are being sent here."

"So what else is new?"

"These two are supposed to be special."

"All Americans think they are special. Remember the one who tried to convince us to share our weapons with whoever was leading the Lebanese government that week?"

Delit snorted.

"So what is these spies' mission here?" asked Zabari.

"We don't know."

"What agency are they from?"

"We are not sure."

"Where do they come from?"

"We are trying to find out."

"Do they have two eyes or three?" asked Zabari in desperation.

"Two," replied Delit, deadpan. "Each. Four, if you add up the total."

Zabari smiled and wagged his finger at his deputy. "All right. What do we know about them?"

"All we know is that they are called Remo and

Chiun and that they are expected here tomorrow morning. And the only reason we know that is the American president told our ambassador as much during a state dinner."

"Why on earth would he do that?"

"Just showing how friendly a new president can be, I guess," said Delit.

"Hmmm," mused Zabari some more, "the trouble with the great number of various spies we have here is that we can never be sure whether any new arrival is meaningless or extremely important."

Delit looked up and his face was grave. "These agents come on orders from Washington. Near where Ben Isaac Goldman was murdered."

The left side of Zabari's face darkened. "And we sit in Tel Aviv, near where Hegez was murdered. I know, Toe, and I will keep this in mind. Put an agent on these two new American agents. I want to know what they are up to."

Delit's face remained grave. "Something seems to be stirring across the sand," he said. "First these murders, then increased transport between the Arab states and Russia, then this Remo and Chiun. I say it is no good. I say it is connected."

Zabari leaned forward, brought his hand up to the right side of his face, then brought it down suddenly to drum on the desk.

"No one is more aware of these things than I. We will keep a watchful eye out, we will cover our asses, and we will follow these two American operatives. If they are indeed related to the security of our ... uh, material, we will take care of them."

Zabari leaned back in his chair and breathed deeply. "Enough of this doom saying. Toe, have you written any new poetry on your vacation?"

Delit's face brightened.

CHAPTER FOUR

"About 2000 B.C.," said the stewardess, "Israel was known as the land of Canaan. The Scriptures tell us that this was a good land, a land of brooks, of water, of fountains, and depths that spring out of valleys and hills. A land of wheat and barley and vines and fig trees and pomegranates; a land of olive oil and honey."

"A land of cheapskates," said Chiun.

"Shush," said Remo.

The jet was circling over Lod airport while the stewardess delivered sightseeing information over the intercom and Remo and Chiun had a deeply motivated religious discussion.

"Herod the Wonderful was a much abused person," Chiun was saying. "The House of David was always plotting against him. The House of Sinanju never got a day's work from the House of David."

47

"But Jesus and the Virgin Mary came from the House of David," said Remo.

"So?" replied Chiun. "They were poor. Royalty yet poor. That shows what can happen to a family that refuses to properly employ an assassin."

"I don't care what you say," said Remo, who was brought up in an orphanage by nuns. "I still like Jesus and Mary."

"Naturally you would. You choose to believe, not know. If everyone was like Jesus, we would starve," declared Chiun. "And since you like Mary so much, did you send it?"

"What?"

"The Norman Lear, Norman Lear message."

"Not yet, not yet," said Remo.

The jet finally received its runway coordinates and was slowly coming in for a landing when the stewardess on the intercom finished up.

"The Israelis have flourished as a nation of farmers and shepherds, of traders and warriors, of poets and scholars."

"Of cheapskates," said an Oriental voice in the back.

Remo had managed to convince Chiun, for ease of movement, to limit his traveling luggage to only two of his colorful, lacquered steamer trunks.

So Remo had to lug only the two trunks onto the Lod–Tel Aviv bus, since the wizened Oriental refused to have them on the roof with the other baggage.

"Baggage?" said Chiun, "Baggage? Are the golden sands merely dirt? Are the fluffy clouds merely smoke? Are the magnificent heavens merely black space?"

"All right, already," said Remo tiredly. So now he sat between two, upright, bouncing trunks as the old bus wound its way through the suburbs of Tel Aviv.

The roads were lined with Y-shaped lights, curling green bushes, and long rows of three-story, tan and gray apartment buildings.

Chiun sat behind Remo, both of them completely level at all times while the rest of the passengers bounced up and down.

"They have let this place go to rot," Chiun said.

"Rot?" said Remo. "Look around. Just a few years ago this was desert and dust. Now it's farmland and buildings."

Chiun shrugged. "When Herod had it, it was beautiful with palaces."

Remo chose to ignore him and watch the scenery. The steamer trunks kept bouncing in and out of his view but he managed to catch the sounds and flavor of Tel Aviv.

Snatches of Hebrew mingled with the aroma of fresh roasted coffee and the tinny noise of American rock and roll on a cheap record player. The guttural Arab hawking of a sidewalk salesman weaved through the thick odor of cooking oil and boiled sweet corn over charcoal on passing street corners.

A drumming, off-tune song drifted in from the other side of the bus as a loaded military truck passed by. Rattling conversations were bursting from every direction. From under canopied balconies, inside cafés, outside espresso shops, beside crowded bookstores. And everywhere, the large bold letters of Hebrew.

The bus passed the rich turquoise of the sea, and the dusty white of new apartment complexes. The hot red and glaring blue of neon lights shot through the gray heat haze and the light green of the Israel spring.

When the bus bumped to a stop in front of the hotel, Chiun left by the back door as Remo struggled through the crowds of excited American teenagers, marked by their expensive jeans and backpacks, middle-aged couples trying to recapture their roots on a two-week vacation and Japanese tourists checking Swiss watches and shooting German cameras at anything that moved.

Remo lowered the trunks to the sidewalk in front of the Israel Sheraton as three smiling men approached from behind Chiun.

"Ah, hello, hello, Mr. Remo. Welcome to Israel, ho, ho," said one dark, smiling face.

"Ah, yes, Mr. Remo," said another smiling face, putting out his hand, "Good to see you and your part . . . I mean, associate, Mr. Chiun."

"We were told to meet you," said the third, "by the American consulate, to take you and Mr. Chiun to a meeting with him right away."

"Oh, yes, oh, yes," said the first. "We have a car awaiting you just around the next corner, ho, ho."

"Ah, yes," said the second. "If you two gentlemen would merely step this way, please, if you would be so kind?"

Remo did not move. He looked at the third man. "Your turn," he said.

50

The three kept smiling, but their eyes darted back and forth. They were all dark-skinned and curly-haired, and wore loud Hawaiian shirts with baggy black pin-striped suits, as if they had confused "Hawaii Five-O" with "The Untouchables."

"Ah, we must hurry," cried the third. "The American ambassador awaits."

"The car, if you please," said the first.

"Around the corner," said the second.

"What about my trunks?" said Chiun.

The eyes darted back and forth again. Remo rolled his skyward.

"Uh, yes," said the third. "They will be taken care of, indeed."

"Well," said Remo, "if the trunks will be well taken care of, indeed, and the American ambassador or consulate or somebody wants to see us, we can't very well refuse, can we?"

"Ah, yes, ah, yes, very good," said all three, ushering Remo and Chiun around the corner in a "V" formation.

"Yes, we can," whispered Chiun. "These men have no intention of taking care of my trunks."

"Ssh," whispered Remo back, "this is a break. We can find out who is behind all these killings from them. Besides, I don't want them shooting up the crowd."

"These men are nothing," Chiun said. "Talk to them and you will get three dead men. Lose my trunks and you will get never-ending guilt."

"As opposed to?" asked Remo. Chiun folded his arms and set his lips in stubborn silence.

Around them, the three men in "V" formation chattered, and Remo called out, "What are you

51

guys? That doesn't sound like Hebrew. You Arabic?"

"Oh, no," said the first.

"No, no, no," said the second and third quickly.

"Ho, ho, ho," they all said.

"We are from Peru," said the first.

"Yes. We are Perubic," said the second.

Remo looked at Chiun and rolled his eyes in disgust. "They're Perubic, Chiun."

"And you are normal," Chiun said.

"What language they speak in Peru, Chiun?" Remo asked softly.

"The interlopers speak Spanish. The real people speak the Quechua dialects."

"And what are these three babbling in?"

"Arabic," said Chiun. "They are talking about how they are going to kill us." He paused, listening to the conversation around them for a moment, then shouted: "Hold. Hold."

The three men stopped short. Chiun let go a short machine-gun burst of Arabic.

"What'd you tell them, Chiun?" Remo asked.

"Insults. Insults. Must I always bear insults?"

"What now?"

"They said they were going to kill us."

"So?"

"They referred to us as the two Americans. I just let them know that you are American as can easily be determined by your ugliness, laziness, stupidity, and inability to learn proper discipline. On the other hand, I am Korean. A human being. This I told them."

"Terrific, Chiun."

"Yes." Chiun agreed.

52

"They'll never guess now that we're on to them, will they?"

"That is not my concern. Protecting the good name of my people from random insults by people who talk in the voices of crows is."

The three "Perubians" were backing away from Remo and Chiun, slowly removing guns from shoulder holsters. Remo sent out a left leg, and the biggest one went skidding down the alleyway, the gun clattering loose from his hand.

The two others stared open-mouthed at the thin American, taking their eyes off Chiun for a fraction of a second. A fraction too long. The next moment, they found themselves hunched in the dirt, deep in the alley, their chins on the ground.

"It is terrible," Chiun said, "when an old man cannot travel anywhere without being threatened with bodily harm. I have no time to play with you, Remo. I am going to sit with my trunks. These awful men with no sense of property have upset me greatly."

Chiun glided away and Remo stepped into the alley. One of the men was stumbling up. His pistol was in his hand. He glared in triumph and pointed it at a gently smiling Remo, then he stared in surprise as there was a tan blur, the gun fired, and the front of his own shirt blew off.

He fell forward muttering in gutter Arabic about fate and fickle gods.

The two men Chiun had pushed into the alley were reaching for their guns too. Remo slapped the guns away and turned one of the men over. He assumed the man was the leader because his suit almost fit.

Remo picked up one of the guns and pointed the barrel at the man's mouth.

"How did you do that to Rahmoud? You were five feet away from him and then his stomach blew all over?"

"I'll ask, you answer," Remo said. He stuck the gun barrel between the man's lips. "Name, please."

The man felt the warm steel between his teeth and saw the look in Remo's eyes. He spoke around the gun barrel. "Achmudslamooncemuhoomoodrazoolech."

"Very good, Ach," said Remo. "Nationality?"

Ahmed Schaman Muhumed Razolie saw his partner rising behind Remo. In his hand was a broken bottle from the alley's dirt floor.

"It is as I said before," he said slowly, stalling for time. "I am from Peru."

"Wrong," said Remo. Without changing his stance, without looking back, he sent a kick behind him. The broken bottle flew into the air and hit the alley's deep dust with a soft thud, followed immediately by Ahmed's partner, who hit with a louder, terminal thud.

Ahmed Razolie looked around the alley at his two dead partners, and then again at Remo, who had just kicked a man's stomach out without looking at him.

"Lebanese," Ahmed said quickly. "I am Lebanese and pleased to welcome you to Israel, melting pot of the Middle East. I stand ready to answer any questions you might have."

"Good. Who sent you?" Remo said.

"No one. No one sent us. We are but simple thieves waylaying a simple pair of American tourists." He remembered Chiun and quickly corrected that. "An American and a human being from Korea."

"Last chance," Remo said. "Who sent you?"

Ahmed saw Allah at that moment. Allah bore a striking resemblance to Muhammad Ali. He was talking to Ahmed.

"Fess up to this American fast,
Or your next breath will be your last.
Give him the news and make it the latest,
And, as you go, Allah's the greatest."

Ahmed was just about to tell Remo of this heavenly vision when his face exploded.

His eyes popped and his cheeks purpled and puffed up. His jaw dropped while most of his hair, left ear, and chin spun back into the alley.

Remo looked at Ahmed's corpse, then turned, straight into the breasts of a dark, brown-haired woman in a khaki uniform.

"Remo Williams?" asked the woman. She pronounced it "R-r-r-emo Weeel-yums."

"I hope so, I'm the only one left standing."

The young woman in the khaki mini and blouse shifted her Uzi submachine gun from her right palm onto her left shoulder, then extended her hand.

"Zhava Fifer, Israeli Defense," she said through rich pulpy lips. "Welcome to Israel. What is your mission here?"

"I'm inspecting your hospitality for the Best Western Motel Chain." He took her hand. It was surprisingly cool for having just blown a man's head apart.

"Enough levity," she said severely. "What is your mission?"

"Are you always this subtle?" Remo asked.

55

"I have no time for games, Mr. Williams," she said, coldly. "As I see it, you owe me your life. You were lucky I arrived when I did."

"As I see it, that's a matter of opinion." He looked around the alley. "Why don't we get away from this party, it's dying anyway, and go some place where you can slip out of your uniform and get comfortable?"

Zhava Fifer took a deep breath. Her uniform, fitted like a second skin, took a deep breath with her.

"My uniform is very comfortable," she said.

Remo looked down at her bosom, only inches away from his chest.

"That's odd," he said.

"What is odd?"

"Your uniform makes me very *uncomfortable*."

"As your people says, 'tough toochis.'" She met Remo's eyes and smiled. "Your Mr. Chiun is waiting for us at the hotel restuarant. There we can talk together."

"Swell," said Remo without enthusiasm. "I can't wait to see Chiun again."

"I would have arrived sooner to save him," Zhava Fifer was telling Chiun, "but I left my magazine in a book stall."

"*National Geographic? Playgirl?*" Remo asked.

"No, Mr. Williams. This one." She touched the clip for the submachine gun, which hung on the back of her chair.

The small restaurant was done in green and orange plastic with red tablecloths, to soak up any blood that might be spilled, Remo decided. In

56

New York City, a uniformed soldier carrying a gun might cause a riot stepping into a restaurant. At the least, his visit would bring the police and a consultation with the restaurant manager. In Israel, in a restaurant built for tourists, soldiers carrying guns and grenades were scattered around, eating and drinking, and no one paid them any attention. Zhava Fifer drew eyes, but only as a woman, not as a soldier.

"May I help you?" inquired a waiter with a deep Israeli accent.

"Why?" asked Remo. "Don't you know me? Everybody else in the country seems to."

"Do you have nice fish?" asked Chiun.

"Yes, sir," replied the waiter. He started to scribble on his pad and said, "Nice-fried-fish."

"No," said Chiun, "I did not ask if you sold grease, only if you sold fish. When I say fish, I mean fish."

The waiter blinked. "You could peel it, sir," he said, hopefully.

"Fine," said Chiun. "You serve me fried fish, I will peel it, then I will drop it all on the floor, and at the end of the meal you will pay me for doing your work for you."

"We'll have two waters," interrupted Remo. "Mineral if you have it, clean glasses if you don't."

"Nothing for me, thank you," said Zhava.

The waiter fled.

"So," said Remo to Zhava. "Who is killing the Israelis and leaving them in the shape of a swastika?"

"If you had been more careful with those men who attacked you, we might have found out."

57

"Sorry," Remo said. "I'll remember not to fight back the next time I am attacked."

Zhava looked deep into Remo's eyes and, to his surprise, she blushed. Suddenly, she looked down and started to pull at her napkin.

"I am sorry," she said. "I know that it was my fault. I—I shot too soon. We were so close to finding out and I, and I . . ."

She rose quickly and ran to the ladies' room. She shot by the waiter, nearly knocking him over, and pounded through the door.

Remo turned to Chiun, who was inspecting the silverware for cleanliness.

"She must really be upset," Remo said. "She left her gun."

The Uzi still hung on her chair.

"Very clever girl," replied Chiun, still intent on the forks, "moments with you and she begins to cry. Very clever. She took from the gun the thing that holds the bullets."

The waiter served the two glasses of water, looking very carefully at Chiun and at Remo, who was checking Zhava's gun. The clip of shells was gone. Remo looked around and saw four Israeli soldiers watching him from other tables, their hands resting on their own guns. Remo sat back. The soldiers relaxed.

Chiun picked up a water glass, examining it carefully. Remo turned toward the lavatory door. Chiun sniffed at the clear liquid. Remo thought there was something strange about Zhava Fifer. Kills a man one moment, starts crying the next. Either extremely unbalanced or a little girl trying to be a big soldier. Or trying to get sympathy. Or trying to escape. Or going to report. Or . . .

58

Remo stopped thinking along those lines. It was getting too confusing.

But there were two facts that were not confusing. First, she had killed Remo's one lead. And two, like Ahmed, in the alley she had known who Remo was.

Zhava was coming out of the ladies' room, eyes dry and head high, when Chiun sipped at the water. The Korean held the liquid in his mouth, looked at the ceiling, swirled it from one cheek to the other, then spat it out.

Looking directly at the waiter, Chiun poured out the water onto the floor.

As Zhava reached the table, Remo was up and handing her the Uzi. "The water maven is displeased," he said. "Chiun, I'll meet you later."

"Good," said Chiun. "See if you can find some good water."

"I think the PLO is behind these killings," said Zhava.

"Who else?" said Remo, who did not know who the PLO was. "I knew all along it was the BLO," he added for emphasis.

"PLO," Zhava corrected. "The Palestine Liberation Organization. Really, Remo, I am amazed at what you don't know."

They were walking along Allenby Road, in front of its more than 100 bookstores where Israeli civilians, soldiers, Arabs, Italians, Swiss, and others bought and discussed the more than 225 weekly, biweekly, monthly, bimonthly, quarterly, biyearly, and yearly editions of Israel's magazines, usually at the tops of their voices. Any discussion here would be indistinguishable from any other, no matter what the topic.

"I'll tell you some things I do know," Remo said testily. "Everybody in this country apparently knows who I am. So much for security. Some have already tried to kill me. I'd say the secret agent business isn't what it used to be."

"I don't know who you are," said Zhava.

"I'm the man who came to protect your atomic bombs," Remo said.

"What atomic bombs?" she asked innocently.

"The ones I read about in *Time* magazine," said Remo.

"Who believes anything in *Time* magazine?" she replied.

"But you do have them, don't you?" said Remo.

"Have what?" Zhava answered gently.

"That reminds me," said Remo. "I've always wondered. Why do Jews always answer a question with a question?"

Zhava laughed. "Who says Jews always answer a question with a question?"

They both laughed, and Remo, said, "Who wants to know?"

Zhava laughed harder. "Who knows?" she said.

"Who cares?" Remo said, and Zhava began to laugh so hard that she soon had tears streaming down her cheeks and was trying to clap her hands together, but kept missing. At last, Remo thought. His opportunity.

He leaned close and whispered in her ear, "I've been sent to protect your bombs. Want to see my big red 'S'?"

Zhava screamed in glee and nearly fell over. Remo smiled and held onto her shoulders as she quaked and shook and got red. Passers-by grinned and gave them plenty of room.

Zhava turned in his hands and buried her head on Remo's chest, hitting his shoulders with her palms and laughing.

"Wooo, hic, ha, ha," she said. "For the, hee, hee, record, hoooo, I know, hic, ha, ha, ha, ha, nothing about, ha, ha, ha, hee, heh, any, hic, atomic, heh, heh, heh, bombs. Hic."

So much for taking advantage of her. Remo continued to smile and pat her back until she calmed down. Suddenly he felt her stiffen under his hands, and she backed off. Remo saw something like dread pass across her face. She was back to being herself again. Zhava Fifer, girl soldier. She hiccupped.

"Tell you what," said Remo. "Let's try word association. You say the first thing that pops into your head."

"Tail."

"Not yet. Wait until I say a word first."

"Second."

"Wait a minute, will you?" Remo laughed. "Now. Home."

"Then—kibbutz."

"Sand."

"Sea."

"Work."

"Play."

"Death," tried Remo.

"Sex," said Zhava.

"Doom."

"Love."

"Bombs."

"Hic!"

61

"Hic?"

Zhava hiccupped again.

"Tell you what. Let's find another place to talk."

"What?" said Zhava.

"Talk," said Remo.

"Dinner," said Zhava.

"What?"

"Dance."

"Dance?"

"Fine," said Zhava. "It's a date. I'll meet you at your hotel later this afternoon."

She blew a forced-looking kiss at Remo, then disappeared into the crowd.

Remo shook his head. Some soldier.

62

CHAPTER FIVE

"The Talmud says, 'The lion roars when he is satisfied, the man sins when he has plenty.'"

"The Talmud also says, 'Chew with your teeth and you will find strength in your feet.'"

"You have stumped me again," Yoel Zabari laughed. "Now, what else does our agent Fifer tell us?"

"That is about all," Tochala Delit replied, "except that she has arranged a further meeting with this Remo and feels more information will be forthcoming."

The two sat in their customary places, papers strewn across Delit's lap and Zabari playing with a plastic photograph cube he had picked up in America. All four sides were filled with snapshots of his children, while the top was reserved for a smiling color print of his wife. Zabari often flipped their images before him while thinking.

"She is a good agent, our Zhava. How does she feel about this assignment?"

"She finds both the American and Oriental eccentric, but sees their potential as, in her words, 'devastatingly effective.' "

"I did not mean that," said Zabari. "I meant her personal standing. Do you think she is ready for espionage work again?"

Delit looked up from his reports. "If you doubt my choice, I can always . . ."

"Of course not, Toe. When have I ever doubted your methods? It is just that . . . Well, Fifer has suffered a great loss," Zabari explained.

"I felt the job would be the best thing for her," said Delit.

"And you are right. Hmmm," Zabari mused. "Have you found any connection between the two dead Israelis and the three terrorists?"

"None," said Delit.

"None?" echoed Zabari.

"Whatsoever," finished Delit.

Zabari stood, his left eye gleaming and the left side of his face flushed. "This is bad. This is very bad. Either these attacks are the most fantastic of coincidences or our enemies are taking great trouble in eluding us." He paced around the office, past his wall of books, his wall of awards and degrees, his wall of family mementos and pictures, then back to his desk again. Zabari picked up his family photograph cube and made the circuit again.

Book wall, award wall, family wall, desk, book wall, award wall. He stopped, flipping the cube, beside a scrawled crayon drawing of a rocket, embossed with a Star of David, blasting toward a green cheese moon.

Below the large construction paper picture was a coarse sheet of lined yellow paper that read, "The Magic Rocket of Peace"—Dov Zabari—Aged Eight—and the teacher's red pencil mark, "A+."

"Keep checking," Zabari finally said, flipping the cube. "There must be a connection."

"Very well," said Delit, "but if you want my opinion . . ."

"Yes, of course, Toe, go ahead."

"I think we should concentrate on these two new spies. This Remo and Chiun. They will lead us to what we want to know. Terrorists we have plenty of. If I continue wasting my time checking, there is no guarantee that we will find out anything."

"True," said Zabari, "but, in life, there are no guarantees for anything. Keep looking. I have a hunch about this. Our American friends are well in hand. You said so yourself. Fifer knows what she is doing. If she needs help, give it to her."

The two talked for another twenty minutes about various legal and archeological matters, including the shipment of new protective security devices, until Delit excused himself and went to the bathroom.

Zabari rubbed the left side of his face and thought about growing half a beard.

CHAPTER SIX

"Petty," said Remo. "Petty, childish, spoiled pettiness."

"Thank you, Remo," said the Master from his mat in between the suite's two beds.

The suite looked like every other suite in every other Sheraton Hotel all over the world. Remo wanted to get a single since Chiun never used a bed anyway, but the Reservation Desk man would not hear of it.

"How many of you are there?" he asked.

"Of me? One," said Remo.

"No, of your party," said the Reservation Desk man who had a little red and white plasticene name tag that read, "Schlomo Artov."

"Two," Remo said miserably.

"Then you will want a double, correct?"

"No, I will want a single," insisted Remo.

Schlomo got angry. "Do you mean to tell me

that you would deny that sweet old man a comfortable bed to sleep in?"

Chiun, who had been instructing four bellboys, and one bell captain who had the misfortune of being on duty that day, in the fine art of steamer-trunk carrying, swung around.

"Deny? Deny? What are you going to deny me now, Remo?"

"Keep out of this, Little Father," said Remo, turning to him.

"Oho!" cried Schlomo, his righteous indignation really rankled, "So he is your father. And this is not the first time this has happened."

"No," said Chiun, "he has denied me many things over the years. Every small pleasure I request is denied. Remember last Christmas? I ask you, is Barbra Streisand so hard to get?"

"We'll take a double," shouted Remo.

"Well, that is better," said Schlomo, ripping a key from the wall. As Artov handed the key over, Chiun returned to his instructions as if he had never been interrupted.

As Remo signed the register, Schlomo warned, "You had better watch yourself, young man. If you mistreat your father in this hotel, I will have you arrested so fast, it will make your head spin."

Remo finished signing the register as Norman Lear, Sr., and Norman Lear, Jr., then advised Artov, "As long as you're concerned, my father insists upon being called by his full name." Before Artov could reply, Remo was collecting Chiun and the luggage to go upstairs.

"Petty," Remo repeated. "Petty, petty, petty."

"Four thank yous," Chiun replied. "That is the

nicest thing you have said to me since our arrival, Remo."

"What are you talking about?" Remo asked as he started to change into a light blue short-sleeved shirt and tan slacks he had bought in the states and sneaked in between two of Chiun's kimonos.

"I know," said Chiun sagely. "You compare me to the great American who goes quickly in circles to destroy ugly pollution machines. It is not much of a compliment. But for an American with so little worthwhile to compare me to, it suffices."

Remo felt as if he were going in circles too. "I've got big news for you, Little Father. I don't know what you're talking about."

"That is not news, Remo. Heh, heh, heh. That is not news. But I thank you because you know that I too try to destroy pollution. I pour out tainted water when it is filled with dangerous amounts of magnesium, copper, mercury, iodine, toxic alloys . . ."

The truth finally struck Remo. "Petty. Right. Petty. I don't mean Richard Petty, the race driver. I mean petty, the word. Meaning small, trivial, shallow, chintzy, nit-picking."

"Because I try to do what is right and good, you throw words at me. With a female at your side, even tainted water in your stomach is of no importance to you. When will my efforts be recognized?"

"Don't worry," said Remo, slipping on the brown loafers he had worn to Israel. "I'm sure they've been heard all over the hotel by now."

"Good. It is good that they know," said Chiun,

69

settling down on his mat and turning on the suite's television set.

"And I've got more news for you," said Remo, going to the door. "That female happens to be an Israeli agent."

Chiun turned. "As we met in Hollywood?" he asked excitedly. "Can she get me good water?"

"No, not that kind of agent. A secret agent, like me."

"In that case," said Chiun turning back, "she is no agent of mine."

Remo opened the suite's door. "I'm going out to make a call. This phone might be tapped. Want anything?"

"Yes," said Chiun, face intent on the screen, "some good water and a son who recognizes undying effort."

"I'll look for water," Remo said.

Remo drifted down the access road that serves as a kind of beach-front driveway for all the hotels on Tel Aviv's Mediterranean shore.

On this spring day, thousands of people were crowding the beaches of Israeli's "Miami," so Remo simply watched the groups of tourists dragging beach chairs, teenagers running with surfboards, and venders hawking ice cream and popsicles. Off the boardwalk, some soldiers were batting at a rubber ball, with frenzied determination, making it look like a red pole and sound like a locomotive.

Remo looked beyond all this, trying to spy a phone. He had not raised his body temperature to match that of the 105-degree air around him, because he wanted to sweat. In case Chiun had not merely been complaining about the water, he wanted to get its poisons out of his body quickly. He wiped the water from his forehead as he moved past the crowd onto Hagarkon Road and arrived at the main shorefront strip of Ben Yehuda.

Still no phone. Remo moved down a block to Keren Kayemet, where he asked a passing old man, "Telephone?"

The old man raised a weak arm and gestured down the hill along Ben Yehuda, indicating quite a distance and saying, "Shamma."

Remo continued on his way, enjoying the suntanned passersby and the outdoor cafés with their colorful umbrella tables. That is, he enjoyed them for five blocks, and then he began to get impatient.

He stopped a passing tourist, "Do you know where Shamma is?"

Remo guessed that the man with meat on his breath and fat on his belly was a tourist because of the two cameras, a binocular case, and a Mexican tequila medallion that were hanging from his shoulders.

"Shamma?" the tourist said, bathing Remo in the scents of yesterday's falafel, a purse-shaped sandwich of dough filled with deep fried, mashed, chick pea meatballs. "Let's see now."

The tourist unzipped his binocular case and pulled a map from between a bottle of vodka and a bottle of orange juice. He unfolded it across Remo's chest and began to read out loud.

"Judea, Samaria, Gaza, Sinai, Golan, Safed, Afula, Tiberias, Hedera, Nathania, sounds like the roll call for the goddamn Mickey Mouse

Club, don't it, buddy? Ramleh, Lydda, Rehebot, Beer-Sheba. Nope, can't find no Shamma here. Want me to check the Arab map, mister?"

"Thanks, but no thanks," said Remo, moving away from the map on his chest.

"Sure, buddy," said the man, folding the map badly. "Any time."

Remo crossed Allenby Street and there, finally, in Mograbi Square, was a phone booth.

The phone looked about the same as the non-push-button variety back home except for the slanted glass tube just above the dial, which Remo was trying to slip a dime into. The phone was not having any. Remo then tried a dollar bill. Nope. He wondered if he could sign for the call. Probably not. Would the booth take a check? Not likely. Remo then considered how the Jewish Momma Bell would like a floating punch right in the receiver.

In the old days in Newark, when Remo and his pals wanted to make a call and nobody had a dime, Woo-Woo Whitfield would always hit the phone casing a certain way and the dial tone came on. Remo tried to remember how and where he hit it. Was it just above or just below the dial? Remo laid an effortless flat-edge slap across the metal housing, which elicited a high-pitched squeal from a small Arab boy who had appeared on the curb next to the booth.

Too bad, thought Remo. He never could beat Woo-Woo at anything, anyway. The Arab kid was shaking his head. "No, no, no," the boy said carefully.

Remo glanced down in his direction. "Not,

now, kid, unless your name is Woo-Woo Whitfield."

Actually, the boy's name was Michael Arzu Ramban Rashi, and like Woo-Woo Whitfield, he was a master at what he did.

Some Arab men tried to be great fighters. Some tried to be great talkers and followers of Allah. Others even tried to live in peace in the Israeli occupied land, but none could match Michael Arzu at doing what he did best. Ramban Rashi was the finest 10-year-old tourist cheat Israel had ever seen.

The dark boy with the face of a greasy Arab angel hung around the seafront environs waiting for marks like the untanned American in the phone booth. Michael began his career selling maps, that he had drawn himself, of an Israel that did not exist. After creating incredible traffic foul-ups with that racket, he moved on up to hawking cups of ice cream with no ice cream in them. Graduating from that fix, Michael developed a talent for monetary exchange.

Ramban Rashi had come to the rescue of many a tourist who had found that he did not have enough Israeli currency to cover a check. Michael Arzu was kind enough to exchange their foreign money for the needed cash. All at a 300 percent rate of profit.

Michael Arzu was waiting for his credit-card machine from the black market, but he already accepted American Express Traveler's Checks.

Michael Arzu Ramban Rashi was enjoying Remo's displeasure immensely. He reached into his own pockets and pulled out a handful of what looked like silver subway tokens.

73

"Simmonim," the boy pronounced. "Telephone tokens," he then translated for the stupid tourist.

"Not shamma?" asked Remo. Michael stepped back a bit to protect his valuable treasure. "Simmonim," he repeated, grinning.

Remo looked carefully at the tokens. They were small, with round holes in the middle. "Metal bagels for the phones," Remo grumbled, pulling a $5 bill from his pocket.

But Michael Arzu shook his head fiercely and closed his hand around the goods.

Remo smiled pleasantly and produced a $10 bill from his pants. Michael shook his head, leering at the coins in his hands like a midwestern teenager with his first pack of dirty playing cards.

Remo took out a $50 bill and waved it at the boy.

Michael Arzu moved forward and with the speed and experience of a professional, plucked the bill from Remo's hand, dropped three simmonim, then raced away, laughing.

For two yards.

Then his feet were pointed straight up, his body was upside down, and his head hung a foot over the sidewalk.

His laugh turned into a frightened scream, then a string of choice expletives from many lands, as Remo, holding onto both his ankles, shook him out. The multilingual obscenities continued as pounds, francs, dollars, yen, agarots, IOUs, coins of all shapes and sizes, can openers, a few watches, fans, and monopoly money began to come down off Ramban Rashi's body.

Before Michael could start productively

screaming for the police, he was on his feet again. Remo had already collected what simmonim there were, while several passing children were making short work of the rest of the spoils.

"That's a good old American shakedown," Remo announced. "When I was your age, I was rolling drunks." He saluted and turned toward the phone. Michael pushed through the children and aimed a vicious kick at the back of Remo's parting knee.

Suddenly Michael found himself gently floating over the other children in the opposite direction. All without the aid of his own legs, which were pointed out behind him. He fully enjoyed the euphoria of flight and watched the passing environment, which included several posts, a fence, and a jeep being driven in the opposite direction by a beautiful brunette. Then Michael met a curly thorn bush and came back to his senses. It was not the beginning of a beautiful friendship. It would be some time before Michael Arzu Ramban Rashi went out of his way to help a tourist again.

Remo began to feed the silver tokens into the phone until they completely filled the slanted glass tube. He dialed "O." A few seconds passed. Then a few more. Then some more. Several more seconds passed after that. Following this, a few more passed, followed by a few more.

Finally a voice came on the line and asked if she could be of assistance. In Hebrew.

Remo said, "What?"

The operator replied in kind. "Ma?"

Which was when Zhava Fifer pulled up to the curb in a jeep. "I have been looking for you,"

75

she said. "I saw a small Arab boy fly by. Was he a suspect of yours?"

"Never mind," replied Remo. "Do you speak the language here?"

"Yes," said Zhava.

"Good," said Remo, handing her the phone. "The operator thinks I'm her mother."

On Remo's instructions, Fifer asked for the overseas operator, then handed the phone back to Remo, explaining that "ma" means "what."

"Thanks," said Remo, looking her over while he was being connected. She was wearing another khaki shirt and mini skirt, but both seemed tighter and shorter than before, if that was possible. Her deeply tanned arms and legs were exposed, plus an ample portion of cleavage. Remo was glad he was not enough like Chiun to think of her as just a female. Damn it, she was a woman. Her hair was down across her shoulders and shone as if just washed. Her lips were a deep rose without lipstick, and she looked remarkably fresh, considering the heat.

Remo decided to take her on a little trip to Shamma, once he found out where the hell that was.

"Overseas operator, may I help you?" said a voice in Remo's ear. Remo replied yes, then gave her Smith's number for that week. The operator promised to connect him, so while he waited, he looked at Zhava as she leaned against the booth. Her left breast was pressed up against the glass so that the tan of her shirt and brown of her skin and the green of her eyes made a fascinating landscape panorama.

"Zhava," said Remo, "where's Shamma?"

Zhava looked quizzically at Remo for a moment, then replied, "There."

"Where?" asked Remo.

"There," repeated Zhava.

"You're not pointing anywhere," said Remo, "Where's there?"

"Shamma," answered Zhava.

"Yes," said Remo, "I'd like to take you there."

"Hello?" came a distant voice. Even though it was very low volume, it still cast a pallor halfway across the world. Remo did not mind, the interruption took his mind off the incredible confusion he had just created.

"Hello, Dr. Smith, head of the super-secret organization, CURE."

The silence was deep and unfathomable. When the reply finally came, two simmonim had been consumed by the phone.

"I do not believe you," came the voice of Smith, registering somewhere in the vicinity of shock, anger, exasperation, exhaustion, and citrus fruit.

"Don't worry, Smitty, even if someone is listening in, which I doubt since this is a public phone, who'd believe it?"

"Anybody who watches television," was the reply. "What do you have for me?"

"An ulcer, an invitation to shamma, which is there, and the names of three freaks who tried to kill us as soon as we arrived."

"Oh, my," Smith sighed wearily. "Who were they?"

"Just a minute," said Remo as three more telephone tokens disappeared into the machine.

"What were those names?" he asked Zhava. "You know, the LPO."

"PLO," she corrected. As she spoke each name, Remo repeated it into the phone.

"Who is that?" asked Smith. "It doesn't sound like Chiun."

"That's because it wasn't. That was an Isareli agent who knew just where to find me when I landed here and just what my name was and just where I came from. She wants to know my mission here. Can I tell her?"

Smith replied as if he were speaking with his head on the desk. "Remo. Try to control yourself. Please?"

"No sweat. I only tell my very best friends. Have you got anything for me?"

Smith breathed deeply a few times before replying. "Yes. The special devices we discussed, you will find them beneath a sulphur extraction plant near Sodom in the Negev desert. It might be worth taking a look. I'll check out your three friends."

Smith broke the connection with audible relief as the last simmonim disappeared. Remo smiled at Zhava and stepped out of the booth.

"That," she said hesitantly, "what you said on the phone. Was that true?"

"Sure," replied Remo. "I'm a secret agent and Chiun is the world's greatest assassin and taught me everything I know, and together we could make a nuclear bomb look like a sparkler."

"You Americans," Zhava laughed, "always with the stories."

CHAPTER SEVEN

Their jeep was racing across the dunes of the Negev desert due southeast toward the Dead Sea. Zhava bounced about, too busy trying to keep from falling out to notice that both Remo and Chiun remained level in their positions, seemingly oblivious to the jolting.

"It was awful," said Chiun from the back of Zhava Fifer's gray army jeep. "There was this wild man shouting English nonsense, and then they sang a song. Barbarism."

"That sounds like the afternoon English lesson telecast from Tel Aviv University," Zhava said. "I got my ooooh . . . ," there was a few seconds pause while she regained her seat, " . . . start on your language from that show."

"My language?" said Chiun, "There is no need to be insulting."

"Come to the point, Little Father," said Remo

from the driver's seat. "What was so bad about the show?"

"Ignorance is no excuse for enjoyment," reported Chiun, "You must be aware of all the facts before I tell you the ultimate barbarism."

Remo and Zhava had picked up Chiun outside the Sheraton, where he stood under a frail bamboo and paper umbrella in the middle of the rush-hour traffic. Since then, he had been haranguing the two about the poor quality of Israeli television.

"There is no daytime drama. There is no poetry. There is no beauty. There are only funny-looking men singing about ... oh, it is too barbarous for me to think about."

Zhava perked up. "I know! I know! I remember the song now. It was about the perfect hamburger!"

She giggled girlishly, Remo laughed, and Chiun's face froze in an expression of disgust.

"Poor young thing," he said. "And I had thought there was hope for you. There is no such thing as the perfect hamburger."

"Uh-oh," said Remo.

"That's true," said Zhava. "But I have tasted a few very good ones in my time."

"I can tell," said Chiun, sniffing the air.

"Leave it alone," said Remo.

Chiun would not be deterred. "Soldier in skirts, I will say this only once and for your own good."

Zhava glanced at Remo, who shrugged. "This'll be the only thing he ever said just once. Pay attention."

"Pay attention," instructed the Korean, "to the age-old wisdom of Sinanju."

Zhava paid attention.

"There is no such thing as a perfect hamburger. There is no such thing as a good hamburger. There is such a thing as a poisoning, destructive, terrible hamburger. The book of Sinanju says, 'That which fills the Universe I regard as my body and that which directs the Universe I regard as my nature.' I do not choose to fill my Universe with hamburger."

"Very wise," intoned Remo.

"Nor do I choose to fill my Universe with useless television programs on reading, writing, and common sense."

"Those shows are not useless," Zhava cried. "Our children need to learn common sense." She turned in the seat to meet Chiun's cold hazel eyes.

"You have more than a dozen countries surrounding you, united in the hope of your destruction," he said. "You have nothing to offer the world but hope and love, so the world abandons you. Your children live in a desert, trying with all their hearts to make it a garden. You are a beautiful young woman who should be carrying a child and wearing royal robes. Instead, you carry a gun and wear the colors of the Army. And you talk to me of common sense."

Zhava opened her mouth to reply, then shut it tightly, looking straight ahead. Chiun looked out across the passing Negev. Remo drove the rest of the way to Sodom in silence.

81

On the southeast tip of the Dead Sea, they found the sulphur extraction plant, a town-sized site encompassing hundreds of square miles of piping, chemical tanks, mineral silos, transport vehicles, all visible, and a nuclear reactor with a fissionable center under twenty feet of prestressed, reinforced concrete, buried invisibly deep beneath the desert sand.

Remo and Chiun stood atop a dune five hundred yards from the first pipe.

"The young hamburger eater sits in the vehicle five miles away," said Chiun, "I have walked with you these five miles in silence. Why have we stopped?"

"Because we are here," said Remo.

"Where?"

Remo tried to figure out an explanation that Chiun would accept, then repeated, "Here."

That seemed to be enough. "That is good. Now what are we doing here?"

"We are going to check this place to see if it's secure."

"Why?"

"Because if it isn't, the whole world may be in trouble," Remo replied testily.

"And how are we to know if it is not secure?"

"By infiltrating it."

"That is truly most wise. I see now that I have walked these five miles with a true genius," Chiun said.

"There you go again. What is it, now?"

"If you succeed in infiltrating, the area is not secure. If you do not succeed in infiltrating, you will be dead. Tell me how you win this game."

Remo looked across the sands toward the sulphur plant. His widened pupils took in the early evening area, which looked as strange and bleak as a massive hunk of moon.

"Everything has got to be perfect for you," he said. "Petty, petty, petty."

Remo walked across the sand to the closest perimeter fence. Chiun shrugged and followed, muttering in Korean how even a Master could not create a tiger's fur from the pasty film covering a white man's body.

"This is probably an electric detector," Remo said of the first fence, looking at the obstructions further on.

"It detects electrics?" asked Chiun.

"No, it detects people through electricity," replied Remo. Fifty meters across the sand were evenly spaced metal posts, three meters apart from each other, but otherwise, unconnected by wires or steel crosspieces of any kind.

"Bah," said Chiun, "this is not a detector. Where is its magnifying glass? Where is its lollipop? It is certainly no American detector."

"You're thinking of a detective," said Remo. "Come on."

The American leaped easily over the fence.

"First I walk, then I am called names, now I am ordered about as if I were a Chinese servant. I will not go. You must lose all by yourself." Chiun settled into the lotus position outside the first fence.

Remo was about to argue, but then shrugged.

"Suit yourself," he said, walking away.

"Take as much time losing as you wish," came Chiun's voice. "I will see if the fence detects me by the time you return."

83

Remo walked toward the second fence, his eyes focusing one hundred meters beyond to the third major obstacle. It appeared to be a simple series of concertina wire—three rows of curled, barbed strands—connected by steel pyramids and backed up by what looked like a deep, metal slit trench. The kind used for troops with light armor.

But there were no troops that Remo could see, just a few small groups of construction workers dotting the area far beyond the slit trench. Since it was night and the workers were without several decades of Sinanju training, their own eyes could not be adjusted to see the thin, thick-wristed, American walking toward them in his blue shirt, tan slacks, and bare feet.

Remo noticed twelve transport dump trucks facing in his direction as well, when he stopped just outside the seemingly unconnected fence posts.

Remo raised his eyes to cover the sulphur plant itself, which sat like a huge, sleeping monster, another one hundred meters back from the loading area, its tentacle-like towers reaching into the sky.

Remo returned his attention to the second group of uprights. Along two sides were a series of carefully drilled holes, interspaced between highly polished, rectangular pieces of metal, fused at various angles to the supporting post. It looked like a personnel barrier that was yet to be completed.

Remo stepped back and looked over the entire area, trying to decide what to do. He could leap over the poles, but perhaps the rods were air detectors. He could lob a small stone or some sand between two uprights and see what happened, but that might be like standing in front of a pay cannon. He could simply walk through as if the poles did not exist, but that might have the same effect as interrupting Chiun during his soap operas.

As Remo pondered the situation, Chiun sat back beyond the first perimeter, watching his trainee's progress. He saw that Remo was preparing to leap over the mystifying obstacle. A wise choice, he thought. For the scene looked different in the Master's older, sharper eyes. Not only did Chiun see the uprights three meters apart from one another, but he also saw the criss-crossing light patterns of infrared laser light. Not only did he see trucks and workers, but he also saw the small arms weapons stacked in shadow under the truck's bodies, and the laced military boots that stuck out of the bottoms of their mechanic's overalls.

Remo did not think to check for the infrared light beams that bounced from pole to pole all along the line of the second perimeter, as he brought his right foot off the ground. With a simple flex of his left leg muscles, he was off the sand and floating through the air.

But the jump was incorrect. Chiun saw that. Instead of a simple upward leap, Remo had moved forward slightly, causing his left foot to push a small cloud of sand across the beams of dim red light just before he left the ground.

The only sound was of a bird chirping. The only movement, besides Remo's soundless landing, was Chiun's silent take-off.

The refinery exploded into life. The recorded

85

signal of the chirping bird sent the workmen scattering. Suddenly, four high-powered, infrared searchlights beamed on from high atop the refinery towers, splashing the entire area with an eerie, bloody glow. Remo was picked out of the landscape like an ant in a bowl of vanilla pudding.

But only for a second. Then he was off and moving, so all the spotlights saw before six hydraulic lifts raised their mounted fifty-caliber submachine guns to a height of one-half meter above the sand, was a tiny Oriental in a golden kimono appearing to float across the sand toward them.

The guns began firing according to their automated, pre-fed systems. As the fifties sent crossfire patterns whistling over the sand, Remo heard Chiun's voice roar above the sound, "Dove's wings," and suddenly he was airborne.

"Dove's wings" was based on the conceit that the white bird of peace could always fly above any conflict, thereby avoiding injury. For Remo the technique was different, but the outcome was the same. As the first bullets were fired, Remo's brain registered the fire power and pattern, then he moved in perfect synchronization with the guns so that his legs were always above where any lead sped at any given moment.

At the end of one running "L" circuit, Remo heard his Master's voice instruct, "Down." Remo slid to the ground as easily as a feather floating to earth.

Beside him lay Chiun.

"Hi," said Remo, "What's a nice person like you doing in a place like this?"

"Doing all your seeing for you," replied Chiun, "although I do not see why I bother. Not only are you blind, but you jump badly. Even the lowly animals of the field can jump. From you, I merely expect competence. I see now that is too much."

Remo pushed his face into the sand as a bullet whined past, a quarter of an inch above his head.

"How was I to know it was an infrared fence?" he asked.

"You have eyes, do you not? To mistake material surroundings for true reality is to mistake a buffoon for your son. We have both made mistakes."

As the two chatted flat on their faces, a crew of men pulled canvas covers off the dump truck holds. The drivers raised the trailer mechanisms for a higher point of view. Inside the hold of each truck was a machine that looked like a rocket launcher attached to a television camera. All twelve trucks lifted their payloads to maximum height, then the men left the cabs and canvas covers and ran to the slit-trench.

The machine gun stopped firing, and suddenly there was silence.

"Uh-oh," said Remo as the machine gun's harsh echoes died away. "What now?"

"Do not ask me," said Chiun, "for I am petty. Merely secondary to your own wondrous abilities. Wondrous one, why not stand up and find out? Simply ignore my ignoble, shallow, trivial self, and leap badly to your feet again."

"Okay, okay, I'm sorry," said Remo. "See? I've apologized. Now if you don't mind, I'm getting out of here."

"Why should I mind?" said Chiun. "I am only of secondary significance."

"I said I was sorry," said Remo, who was up and running.

Suddenly the dump truck closest to the American's running figure boomed and a four-foot, roaring projectile was following Remo. Back at the truck, the television camera picked up and focused on him with its sensitive heat-seeking equipment.

Remo started to zigzag, but the camera followed him, and the missile began to zigzag as well, lighting up the area with orange flame.

Aha, Remo thought, picking up speed and turning around, so this is a TOW device. Smith had told him of the American-made Television Operated Weapon during a debriefing a few years back. Only he had not mentioned that they were now being put to use by the Israelis. Remo considered racing the missile back to Sodom, but he did not want any suburbs exploding, so he doubled back again, this time heading straight at the first dump truck.

But he had to make it across the third perimeter's barbed-wire fence. As Remo jumped over the first row of curled, pointed metal, the projectile was twenty-five feet behind him.

As he took the second row, Remo could hear only the roaring of the rocket and was hoping that these leaps were not cutting down his speed too much.

As he went over the third, the cone of air that had accumulated in front of the missile's tip pressed against Remo's back.

With a final shot of speed, Remo ran directly at

the TOW launcher. To any Israeli looking, it seemed as if he were about to be sandwiched between the truck and the explosive charge.

At the last moment, Remo lowered his body temperature to the point that he did not exist for any heat-seeking device, and fell to the sand.

The first dump truck exploded in a ball of orange-black flame, hurling metal, plastic, and garbage across the plant and into the desert for miles around.

The sulphur plant soldiers, who were very busy keeping the fire from spreading to the other weapons, called it a miracle. The Israeli military, who combed the desert for any sign of enemy commandos or charred bodies, called it crazy. Yoel Zabari and Tochala Delit, who were roused from sleep and were that close to calling a full military alert, had a few very choice words for it. And Chiun, who had been waiting amid rubble outside the first perimeter fence when Remo trotted up with a smug grin on his face just seconds after the explosion, had a word for it, too.

The word was "litterbug."

CHAPTER EIGHT

The dark shape moved silently across the Israeli night sky. From Jordan it came, low and deadly. Not like a jet, which sent out sound warnings even before it crossed the border. Not like a Phantom fighter, which would be shot down immediately by the Israeli border defense.

No, it came like the silent wind, because it was a transport glider. Soundless, flying too low for radar, painted black to merge with the night desert sky, it moved invisibly into the Negev.

Abulicta Moroka Bashmar paced before his men, dressed in an antiradar plasticene scuba suit with specially made antiradar plasticene medals affixed on his chest.

"This is the moment," he said in English to the three men lined up by the door of the glider in their scuba suits and parachutes. "So far the Israeli patrols have not detected us. We will parachute into their Dead Sea, kill as many of them as possible, then swim back into Jordan and return to our own lands."

The three men smiled, secure in the knowledge of Bashmar's reputation for bravery, a reputation that he had acquired after leading fifty Libyan terrorists into an unguarded Israeli schoolhouse and massacring the eighty-three students and thirty-seven teachers within. The men were sure that this mission would be as satisfying. One of the men was black, a special commando recruited from Uganda.

Bashmar raised his hand. "Drop our equipment . . . now." His hand chopped the air, and the black commando, nearest the open door, nudged the plasticene carrier with its underwater gear out.

"Now, we go," cried Bashmar as he fell out of the glider door, clutching a plastic-enclosed machine gun to his plastic-enclosed chest. The three others followed, and soon four dark figures and one dark thing were plummeting through the Israeli night sky.

First, the dark silk parachute for the equipment opened, and then each man pulled his rip cord. Each man's mind was filled with the visions of the violence they would create and the rewards they would receive on returning home to Libya and to Uganda.

Bashmar's brain thought of the honoring military welcome and promotion he would receive. The hard part was over. They had infiltrated Jordan, crossed into Israel, now all they had to do was massacre and leave.

Zhava Fifer was dozing in the jeep when she heard the explosion coming from the Dead Sea.

The commandos' underwater equipment hit the highest-density water in the world from a height of three thousand feet, and the resulting sound clap rivaled that of a grenade.

The first explosion woke her. The next four sent her scrambling for the car keys and wheeling the jeep in the direction of the shore.

Bashmar and his troops were bobbing like corks on the surface of the salt-thickened water.

When Zhava arrived at the Dead Sea, a dark figure was slapping two other dark figures with a dark rubber flipper.

"Idiots! Fools!" the figure was saying in accented English. "You are useless. Why did you not tell me that we could not swim in this? We will have to float back to Jordan."

"I thought he knew," said one figure, pointing at the other.

"I thought he knew," said the other, pointing back.

As soon as she heard the Arab accents, Zhava reached for the Mauser automatic pistol she kept under the dashboard in a specially disguised holster. But just as she touched it, a hard, round, metal rod dug into the back of her neck, accompanied by a low laugh.

"Commander," said a high-pitched voice behind her, "I got us a woman."

Bashmar dropped the scuba fin and tried to peer through the darkness for the Uganda soldier. He came forward, trailed by the two other Libyans, until he was beside the gray jeep.

"I kill this bitch in your name," said the voice behind Zhava. "She will know she dies at the hands of . . ."

93

"Wait," said Bashmar.

All this time Zhava had remained motionless, her sitting torso arched, her breasts jutting forward. Bashmar took in the full view of her deep cleft and the swelling sides of her round breasts.

"Oh, ho," he said, leaning down to caress one dark, smooth leg.

Zhava tried to move back, but the hard metal on the back of her neck would not yield. "Move or scream and I will cut off your head," Bashmar said.

Bashmar moved his other hand across Zhava's shoulder. "This will be our first victim of the night," he said, pulling off his rubber head cover. The two behind him followed suit. Zhava's breathing became deeper, making the view down her shirt even more enticing. She felt the gun barrel move away from her neck and then heard the soldier behind her disrobing.

"But first," said Bashmar, eyeing her bosom, "you will feel the strength of the Arab body and the might of the Arab mind. You will witness the superiority of our culture."

"Ours, too. Africa," said the voice behind her. "I a colonel."

Bashmar ripped Zhava's shirt off.

His men looked like they were on the verge of applause. The man behind Zhava's neck leaned over her shoulder for a look. Zhava closed her eyes and tried to squeeze the tears back.

Bashmar pulled a silenced automatic pistol out of a plastic bag, then stuck it under Zhava's left breast, pushing her backward across the two front seats. The standard shift stick dug into the

94

small of her back. Zhava bit her lip, her mind filling with humiliation and hatred.

Suddenly the gun that had been on her neck was under her chin, and two pairs of hands gripped her legs. She tried to scream but a rubber head piece was stuffed into her open mouth.

"To the greater glory of the Arab world's fight for freedom. And Africa's," said Bashmar, who then unzipped the pants of his scuba suit. Zhava felt a gun barrel pry at the buttons of her skirt. The only sounds she could then hear were the squeaking of rubber as she ground her teeth, the roaring in her head, and the unsnapping of buttons.

Yellow haze drifted across her vision as the gun barrel was jammed tighter against her throat. She felt the warm night air flow across her exposed crotch. She tried to kick out, but her legs were still tightly held. The last thing she heard before the scream was her panties being ripped off.

At first she thought the scream was her own, but then she felt the stinking rubber of the head cover still in her mouth. Suddenly the pressure under her chin was gone and she heard a short chatter of silenced submachine-gun fire. She found she could sit up, so she sat up and saw a terrorist on his knees staring at the place where his hands should have been. Instead, on the end of his arms were two gushing streams of blood that were messing up Zhava's right leg.

Zhava found that her left leg was free as well, since the other terrorist had his hands full trying to keep the inside of his neck from pouring out.

She saw the yellow blur slide between the two

men, then circle past a confused Abulicta Moroka Bashmar, who stood with his rubber pants down.

Zhava quickly reached under the jeep's dashboard, grabbed her Mauser and shot between Bashmar's legs. The Arab commander's lower middle exploded, spinning out his front and back. Bashmar's face held a dawning awareness of his own mortality as he crumbled over onto the wet sand.

There was silence. Zhava turned unsteadily around and saw the fourth terrorist, or what was left of him, since the Ugandan colonel had somehow managed to stick his machine gun up his own nose and fire.

She pulled the rubber gag from her mouth and looked over the windshield. Remo and Chiun stood in front of the jeep. Chiun had his arms crossed, his hands deep in the sleeves of his golden kimono. Remo leaned casually on the hood, blowing on the fingernails of his left hand.

Zhava Fifer wrapped her torn skirt around her, then fell back into the driver's seat and whistled.

"Welcome back," she said.

Zhava remained silent for quite a long while as Remo drove back to Tel Aviv. Finally, she stirred from her huddled position in the back and said, "You are right."

"Of course," said Chiun.

"I have been thinking about what you said before," continued Zhava, not hearing Chiun's statement, "and you are right."

They had disposed of the bodies themselves, that operation consisting of a shovel, a few rocks,

96

and a large mound of sand, and they were many miles from the Dead Sea.

"I've been thinking about what you said, too, Chiun," pitched in Remo, "And you are right. No one should fill their universe with hamburger or else the Starship Enterprise would have to run on ketchup."

"Ignore the litterbug, young lady," said Chiun, turning in his seat to where Zhava nestled in a blanket in the back. "He is not wise enough to respond to the wisdom of Sinanju."

"The shuttlecraft on onions and pickles," said Remo.

"However," continued Chiun, "your realization of the truth is not sufficient. And an apology does no good."

"Why?" said Zhava. "What have I done?"

"The awful thing you did to that man back there. Disgraceful."

Zhava sat up, her eyes gleaming, her attack of moments before unimportant. "What! You are surprised I killed him? That I shot his disgusting Arab body?"

"No," Chiun replied calmly. "But to shoot him? There is a wrong way of killing, and then, there is Sinanju. I am disappointed. You have shown great promise. Why ruin it with a gun?"

Zhava fell back. "And he talks to me of common sense," she said quietly. She looked out at the desert for a moment, then continued, "You know, you are still right. Why not kill him with my hands? A gun only cheapens what we have achieved in this land with our hands."

Chiun nodded, and Remo leaned over to him.

97

"Not now, Chiun," he whispered. "Let her be. It's not the time."

"Now is exactly the time," replied Chiun. "Go on."

Zhava still stared out to the sands. "This is my home," she said. "This is my father's land. He worked this land and fought for this land and built this land. And it killed him. First inside by fighting a way that became a five-day-a-week job. You do not know what it is like to say goodbye to your family every week for the last time."

Remo turned the wheel to stop by the side of the road. "Keep driving," instructed Chiun.

"That was what destroyed my mother. My mother," Zhava remembered for a moment, "she was a very strong woman. Her only mistake was to love my father more than she loved Israel. When he was blown apart by a Russian-built tank, it left her an empty husk. They could not even find enough of him to fill an envelope. She died three months later."

Zhava laughed suddenly, high-pitched, almost hysterically. "I do not even know why I am telling you this. This is all classified information, you know."

Neither Chiun nor Remo answered.

Zhava lost her smile and stared up at the ceiling of the jeep. "My fiancé, as but a child, worked in the cellar, making bombs. I lost him last month when a terrorist bomb went off. My family and I have always been in the wrong place at the wrong time. Everyone I have ever loved was destroyed by a bomb, and I dedicate my life to protecting . . ." Zhava stopped, without completing the sentence. "I—I am sorry. I have been talking too much."

Remo looked into the rear-view mirror. He saw Zhava's eyes. Empty eyes. Empty of tears, empty of hurt, empty of ghosts. They were the eyes of a professional. No expectations, no dreams, no hopes. They were his own eyes.

"You needn't worry about the bombs," Remo said, trying to reassure her. "They're secure."

"What do you Americans know?" Zhava suddenly flared. "You have a war every twenty years, you fight it on someone else's soil, and then you sit in your easy chairs, and talk about how terrible it was. But war is our way of life. Not just existence. Life. Survival. We are outnumbered three to one, the battles are fought here, on our land, and it is our brothers who are dying. I would kill everyone if it would just end."

Zhava's barely controlled voice rattled into silence. Her eyes drooped and her face grew relaxed. Her speech had been passionate but without any real passion. Passion had been squeezed from her by reality.

Chiun turned to her. "You are upset. Lie back and sleep now."

She did so without complaint. Chiun lay his thin, yellow hands across her brow. "Sleep now. Remember, no paradise in the east, nor in the west. Seek the way you have come. It is within you."

Remo drove along the flat countryside, imagining all the unseen death around him. He drove through high peaks of the North Negev. He drove by moonlike craters in the rocks. He drove

99

past signs saying Hamekesh-Hagodol—The Big Crater. He passed the huge chasm that shone pink, purple, and yellow in the moonlight. Remo's foot pushed down on the accelerator.

"You drive like you jump," said Chiun. "Badly."

"She asleep?" asked Remo.

"I have spent the last ten minutes keeping her awake?"

Remo drove on for a while, thinking about Zhava's last statement. "I would kill everyone if it would just end." He decided not to let her out of his sight. He turned back to Chiun.

"Quite a woman," he said, motioning to Zhava's sleeping form.

"A wise young lady," said Chiun. "I too would be upset if I had killed someone with a gun."

CHAPTER NINE

It was not easy. It was never easy, and it took a long time. But the man knew that soon it would be over and like everything else, all good things were worth waiting for. And working for, and planning for, and suffering for, and killing for.

The thin man of medium height stepped out of the bathroom, naked, after carefully wiping off the toilet and washing his hands. As he walked toward the closet, he dried his hands and his thick wrists. The man stopped before his full-length mirror.

Not bad, he thought. His whole body looked younger than his years. The face lift had done wonders, raising his cheekbones and smoothing out the cruel lines around his brown eyes and thin mouth. Yes, and exercise had kept his body trim, his legs and arms strong, and his carriage and posture correct. As was befitting the man who used to be Major Horst Vessel of the Nazi S.S.

The man who used to be Horst Vessel dressed, thinking about all the good old times in the Fatherland. Germany had key, high-ranking positions for the clever, the educated, the subtle. His present position with the Israeli government proved that. Experience and expertise were always admired, even in the ranks of the heathen. Of course, they had no idea of who he really was and what he used to be.

The man who had been the youngest Nazi officer in a position of power during World War II checked his fully attired appearance.

The next to last thing he did before leaving the room was to drape the Chai on a chain around his neck. The last thing he did was spit on the Hebrew symbol of life.

The thin man with the thick wrists drove his jeep just south of Tel Aviv to a small town named Rehovat. There he found a large, flat, gray building and pulled into the parking lot. He got out of his jeep and went inside.

The man strode down the tiled cellar hallway in disgust. Sweat poured across his proud, straight body. He remembered marching down halls of marble and silk, cool in the German autumn of 1943. He was going to meet, for the first time, the savior of Germany. He was making his first of many visits to the greatest man, the most brilliant tactician, the finest leader the world had ever seen.

It was for that leader that he now slid his Israeli military boots across the unwaxed tile. His neatly groomed head passed just inches below

102

the dull acoustical tile. The drab cinder blocks that were the walls only made the man who had been Horst Vessel long all the more for the glorious paintings, the lush carpets, and the ornate balustrading that he had gloried in during his youth. They had befitted only the greatest.

The man who had been Horst Vessel thought that the environment always befitted the race. No wonder the Jews lived in the desert.

He stopped thinking about the past as he moved by sets of closed wooden doors. He smiled as he heard young voices coming through the cracks in the wall and underneath the doors. Scum. Laugh while you may.

The man who had been Horst Vessel thought about the future. Of a world in black decay. Of nations of chaos. Of the ground under his feet replaced with twisted radioactive waste, and he wanted to laugh in happiness.

He found the room he had been looking for all the way down on the right. The man who had been Horst Vessel opened the door and entered. He stood in a long room filled with lab tables upon which were shelves of chemistry equipment. Each table had a sink on each end and these shelves, which stretched across the table's middle.

At the table farthest from where he stood was another man with his head in one of those sinks.

The man who used to be Fritz Barber was throwing up his guts. All that could be seen of him at the moment was his dirty, flecked lab jacket and his two hands dotted with age gripping the sides of the sink.

The man who had been Horst Vessel clicked his heels loudly in the empty room. The man who

103

had been Fritz Barber continued puking. Lining the tables were surgical instruments: a sharp scalpel, a few rubber gloves, and a metal probe. Beside these operating materials were trays in which seemed to be remnants of a fetal pig.

"I cannot stand it," said the man who used to be Fritz Barber, as he pulled himself out of the sink and sat heavily on the floor. He was a fat, balding man, whose front was spotted with yesterday's dinner. A few, small, liquid green specks littered his chin.

"Are we being listened to?" asked the man who had been Horst Vessel in Hebrew.

"No, no, of course not," said the fat man on the floor whose teacher identification tag read "Dr. Moishe Gavan."

"Then speak German!" the thin man spat harshly, "and rise when a superior officer enters the room!"

"Yes, oh, yes," wheezed the fat man, rising awkwardly to his feet and turning green. He was short and had white hair, not at all like the Fritz Barber of thirty years ago. But now he was Dr. Moishe Gavan, a biology teacher at the Weizmann Institute of Science. Now he taught Jews how to take apart fetal pigs and which disease would cause you to smother in your own waste products and how to tell girls from boys. Times had changed.

"Heil Hitler," the fat man said softly, saluting.

"Heil Hitler," was the crisp reply. "What is all this?"

"Dissections," the fat man smiled weakly, "I am not cut out for this kind of work. I was a physicist in the Fatherland. What do I know of

104

earthworms and crayfish, and frogs and . . ." He began to grow green again.

"You will do as you are told," the thin man said, coming forward, "I have no time for your minor complaints. Do you have it?"

The fat man straightened as best he could and nodded. He still just barely reached the thin man's shoulders. "Yes, of course. That is why I am here. I was supposed to clean up my students' work, but . . ." The fat man became purple.

"Enough," said the man who had been Horst Vessel. "Bring me the device. I do not have all night."

"Yes, yes, yes," said the fat man, then shuffled toward his desk across the room. The man who did not have all night stared down at a neatly drawn and quartered fetal pig without emotion. His hand moved behind his back to settle on a scalpel nearby. As he heard the fat man's labored breathing get nearer, he palmed the surgical knife and slipped it up his sleeve.

The man who was now Dr. Moishe Gavan held a small black box the size of a paperback book in his hands. He carried it as if he were bearing royalty, and his pudgy face was broken up in a proud grin. The fat man held the box up to the taller man.

"That is it?" asked the taller man.

"Yes," came the wheezing reply. "That is as small as I could get it, but still, once it is properly attached, it can detonate a nuclear bomb either by radio signal or by the timing device you see on the side there. It overrides all other safety controls. Turn it on. It cannot be turned off."

105

The man who had been Horst Vessel took the small device from the teacher's hands slowly.

"No need to be so gentle," said the fat man. "It is solid state."

"I am not gentle," the thin man flared. "I am careful." He looked at the box from all sides. "So this will do it, eh?"

"Yes," replied the fat man.

Thirty years of planning. Thirty years of oh-so-careful move and countermove. Thirty years of impersonation and lying. Now it all rushed together inside the man who had been Horst Vessel. Soon he could be Horst Vessel again. Even if only for a few minutes.

"Good," he said. "You have done well. Our plan can now go ahead without delay."

"Excuse me," the fat man began, coming up close, "but what shall I do until I receive my signal to go? I understand why the others had to be killed, but I have done my job. Both the others lost their resolve, but I have stayed until the end. I have done my work. I guarantee it. So, must I stay? Must I continue to teach this scum? Can I not go now?"

The man who had been Horst Vessel looked down, but he did not see the man who had been Fritz Barber. This was not Fritz Barber. Fritz had been clever, he had not been a whiner. He had not been a complainer. He had not been a coward, a runner. This fat man was no German. This man was Moishe Gavan. This man is a Jew.

The thin man smiled. "If you left now, it would create suspicion. Do not worry, old friend, once the final phase of our plan is put into action, you

106

will receive the prearranged signal. Now I must go and prepare for that magnificent moment."

"I understand," mumbled the fat man.

The man who had been Horst Vessel snapped to attention and thrust out his arm in the Nazi salute. "Heil Hitler," he said.

The fat man tried to keep his eyes away from the dissections that lined the table as well as from the thin man's own gaze. He returned the salute. As Gavan's mouth opened to echo "Heil Hitler," the man who had been Horst Vessel slid the scalpel into his uprisen hand and brought it down across the fat man's chest.

The teacher's words stuck in his throat, blocking out any alarm he might have raised, and his eyes popped wide. His arm lowered to about eye level, his legs shook twice, and then he fell forward, blood already spreading across his front.

The man who had been Horst Vessel got down on one knee, then sank the blood-slick scalpel deep into the back of the fat man's neck. The teacher's body jerked one last time. The thin man rose.

The man who had been Fritz Barber had shown an ugly weakening tendency even back then, thought the thin man. I should have recognized it sooner. But no more trouble now. Soon, it will happen. Soon, Hitler's ghost will be satisfied. Soon, the Jews will be dead. All of them.

And if some Arabs had to die as well, then it would be so. It had to be. His purpose was too great to try to avoid destruction of others than the Jews.

The man who had been the youngest ranking

107

officer in the S.S. began to slip on a pair of rubber gloves.

Before I can put the last part of the plan into action, he thought, I must get rid of the American agents.

The thin man then went to find a surgical saw among the laboratory equipment.

CHAPTER TEN

Zhava awoke to the most God-awful racket she had heard since a jet crashed next to her kibbutz when she was a child.

She shot up in the still moving jeep and cried, "What is it? Did we hit a sheep? Have you run over a turkey?"

Chiun turned to Remo. "What is it? Has your terrible driving, that is matched only by your terrible jumping ability, destroyed another living creature?"

"No, Little Father. She's talking about you."

Chiun turned to Zhava. "What was it that you heard, young lady?" he asked gently.

"A terrible high-pitched squealing. It sent shivers up my spine. Ooooh, it was awful."

"There, you see," declared Chiun. "It could not have been me, for I was singing a lovely Korean song that lulled you in your sleep. Tell the truth, now, were you not lulled?"

"Chiun," said Remo, "she is talking about your singing. I thought every Army patrol and wolf pack within twenty miles would be on us any minute."

"What do you know of lull?" asked Chiun. "Just drive, litterbug."

"Drive?" said Zhava. "Was I asleep? Oh, dear, where are we?"

"Be not afraid," said Chiun. "We are in the land of Herod the Wonderful, Israel, on the planet earth."

"But where?" she insisted.

"The map says we have just entered Latrun," Remo said.

"Good," Zhava said. "I was afraid we had missed it. Watch for a turn-off toward Rehovat. I forgot to tell you that we managed to trace the men who tried to kill you. They worked at the Weizmann Institute of Science."

When the trio arrived, they managed to find the Palestinians' rooms without asking. The rooms themselves were unimpressive, unpopulated, and uncluttered by clues. Each was a small, square, cinder-block cell containing a wooden table, a portable wooden closet, a wooden chair, and a wooden canvas-covered cot.

"My people have already gone over the rooms carefully," said Zhava, "but they could find nothing that would lead us to a superior or higher-up."

Chiun had wandered out into the hall as Remo paced up and down the last room, finally stopping by the wooden desk. There he fingered a college textbook.

110

"Did these guys work here or go to classes?"

"Both, actually," Zhava replied. "Their custodial work limited their class time, but they did manage to sit in on several classes. Why?"

"Nothing, really. A biology textbook just wasn't my idea of an Arab best-seller, that's all. I guess that's what this book is."

Suddenly Chiun appeared in the doorway, in each of his hands a book.

"What are you doing?" Remo asked.

"Working," was the reply. "What are you doing?"

"Uh, nothing," said Remo.

"Exactly," said Chiun, dropping the two books to the floor. "While you two were comparing hamburgers you have eaten, I have done your work. Now, see."

Remo looked at the books on the floor. "Really neat, Little Father. They're very nice, but I don't think the institute will let you have them. Why not try the cafeteria? They might let you take something from there."

"You are blind," said Chiun. "You are but looking. I told you to see."

"Wait a moment," said Zhava, getting to her knees. "Did these books come from the other two rooms?"

"Exactly," said Chiun. "Are you sure you have no relatives in Korea?"

Remo looked around the room in confusion. "Somebody tell me what's going on?"

Zhava went to the desk. "Look, Remo," she said, picking up the biology book lying there. "It is the same as the others. See?"

111

"You, too, huh? Okay, I see already. So what?"

"It is a connection. All three Palestinians sat in on the same class each week with the same teacher."

"A second cousin perhaps?" Chiun said to Zhava. "A little training and you could go far."

Remo shot Chiun a nasty look, then kneeled down and flipped open a book. On the inside cover were some scrawled words in Hebrew.

"Here," he said. "What does it say?"

"Biology," Zhava read. "Room B-27. Teacher, Doctor Moishe Gavan."

Remo snapped the book shut and dropped it on the floor with the others.

"Well, let's just go visit Doctor Gavan."

The three moved down the Weizmann Institute hallway toward Room B-27, which was located in the cellar all the way down on the right.

For early morning, the area was abuzz with activity. Many people rushed by the group, most of them older than Remo expected and wearing uniforms. Most of the younger ones were sickly looking, their expressions ranging from grim to green.

"Did we come during a fire drill or something?" Remo asked Zhava.

"Those are not firemen," she whispered. "They are police."

Remo saw a large crowd outside Room B-27, accompanied by a huge stink. He recognized it easily. It followed him everywhere. The stench of death. "Stay here," he instructed Chiun and Zhava. "I'll see what's going on."

"It smells here of pork," said Chiun. "I am go-

112

ing to wait in the vehicle. Tell Remo that," he finished, motioning Zhava on.

Remo had moved through the crowd of teachers and students and was now standing shoulder to shoulder with a burly policeman. The policeman turned toward him and said something impolitely in guttural Hebrew. Remo replied in Korean something about the cop's mother and camel's feet. The policeman said something else, and Remo was about to reply in a more universal language when Zhava appeared by his side, waving a card in front of the policeman's nose and speaking in soothing tones. The policeman lifted his arm and the two moved through.

Zhava and Remo stopped just inside the door of Room B-27 because if they had moved any further, they would have gotten their feet all red.

Completely covering the tile floor was a carpet of blood. In the very center of the room was a gory swastika pieced together from the chubby limbs of what was once a man. All around him were trays of dissected fetal pigs.

"Some people just can't leave their work at the office," Remo said.

Zhava left the room.

Remo looked closer until he saw a small identification card pinned to the upper right hand section of the flesh swastika. It read, "Dr. Moishe Gavan." A guttural voice said something in Hebrew behind him.

Remo turned around to face the policeman and saw Zhava standing behind him. "He wants to know if you are finished," she said.

"Sure," said Remo, "let's go."

They started through the crowd again, Zhava

113

and the Israeli cop leading the way and talking. Remo tapped her on the shoulder.

"Ask him if there is a phone I can use. I've got to report."

"So do I," said Zhava.

"We'll flip for it," said Remo.

Zhava asked, and they were shown to the front office and assured that the line was not tapped. Many important governmental experiments were being tried here, so the security was tight.

Remo won the toss and called Smith. Since it was still very early morning, and there were not many people using the phone at that hour, the overseas connection was made in record time and Remo had to wait only fifteen minutes.

Smith was fresh but less than enthusiastic when he came on the line, especially when he heard about the latest death, of Dr. Gavan.

"You're doing wonderfully," Smith said. "Bodies are piling up all over Israel, and you've blown up a million-dollar weapon ..."

"You heard about that?"

"News travels fast on the war circuit. That nearly caused an international incident right there. Thank heavens no one knows you're responsible. No one does know, do they?"

"I won't tell them if you won't."

"So besides all that, and almost totally blowing your cover, what have you got?"

"A song in my heart and rhythm," said Remo. "Look, Smitty, I don't know what's going on here. That's your job. You find out what blew my cover, you find out the connection between all those dead guys, you find me somebody to do something to."

114

"Easy, Remo, easy," said Smith. "Keep working on it, keep thinking, and I'll get back to you."

"Wonderful," said Remo. "I can hardly wait. Make it quick, and did you send Chiun those tapes? If he doesn't get them soon, he's going to make me into the perfect hamburger."

"The tapes went out yesterday. I know nothing about hamburgers."

"Good. See ya 'round."

Remo hung up in a sour mood. Keep thinking, huh? Well, he had done a little thinking, and he was ready to show that walking answer to the Florida sunshine tree where he could put all his computers.

The facts were simple. Zhava Fifer killed the one lead he had. And everywhere she went, people wound up dead. She was the one, Remo decided. Thinking, huh? How was that for thinking?

He marched out of the front office to where Zhava waited by the door. "Finished?" she asked.

"You betcha," he said. "Your turn."

"Good. I must use the phone now." Zhava moved toward the office.

"Zhava!" Remo called sweetly.

"Yes?" she turned.

"What were you and that policeman talking about before?" Now he had her.

"Nothing, really. Why?"

"Come on, you can tell me. I just want to know." Remo moved in toward her.

"Well, he wanted to know if you had been here a bit earlier. He thought he had seen you here before."

115

A likely story. He'd take her into the office and get the truth out of her. "Oh? And what did you say?"

"I told him no. That you had been with me," Zhava said, then went into the office to use the phone.

Remo stopped and frowned. She couldn't have killed Gavan since she had been with him all night. And how to explain those four dips tackling her in the desert? Remo scratched his head and went outside. He didn't like this thinking bit.

He drifted out into the parking lot where Chiun sat erect in the front seat of the jeep. The sun was just about to rise, highlighting the sand and underlighting rain clouds that spread across the horizon.

Remo leaned against the back of the jeep and wished he could still smoke.

"You are depressed, my son," Chiun said.

"Yeah. This place gets to me."

"It is understandable. It is hard to work in a land of little beauty."

The sun rose, casting a ribbon of colors across the undersides of the the clouds and turning the desert into shimmering gold.

"It's not that," Remo said. "It's just that I haven't gotten anything done."

"Nothing done?" said Chiun. "Last night, you killed two evil men, even though you failed to keep your elbow straight on the back wrist thrust. You call that nothing? Those fools in the alley who endangered my trunks? You have used the skills I taught you. You have used them badly, but, still, is that nothing? Is the thousands of years of wisdom nothing? The shipments of

116

gold in payment nothing? You surprise me, Remo. Several more weeks here and you may yet help solve the overpopulation problem of the cities of this land."

Remo grunted.

"Your discomfort is caused merely by the lack of beauty of this place. Where are the palaces of yesteryear?" Chiun asked.

Remo watched the clouds as they scudded along the horizon, leaving rain-soaked sand in their wake.

"Don't worry about it. Smitty tells me that your shows are on the way."

"That Smith is an idiot," Chiun said. "My beautiful stories will wind up at the Arctic Circle." He paused. "Still, we should return to the hotel to be sure. Now."

When Zhava Fifer walked up, Chiun was dancing back and forth in front of Remo, saying, "Now, now, now."

"What is wrong?" Zhava asked Remo.

"He's about to find out if Brenda's tumor is malignant, if Judge Faithweather has lost his seat on the bench because of his indiscretion with Maggie Barlowe, defense attorney, and whether Doctor Belton's drug rehabilitation therapy will work on Mrs. Baxter's little girl in time for her to ride in the big race."

"What?"

"Never mind. He's just anxious to get back to the hotel."

"Can we send him back with the police?" Zhava asked.

"If they're willing to hear about how marvelous

117

'As the Planet Revolves' is, I don't see why not," Remo said.

"What?"

"Never mind again. Sure, let the police bring him back."

Remo brought Chiun over to the waiting police car and the Korean happily sank into the back seat, babbling about how great Rad Rex, the star of "As the Planet Revolves," was.

"He is truly without peer," said Chiun as the car door closed.

"A marvelous artificer. I have met him. In Hollywood. Yes, it is true. Would you like to see an autographed picture? I have one. He gave it to me personally. I taught him how to move . . ."

Remo and Zhava watched the car move away and the two policemen within turn to each other, saying, "Ma? Ma?" And Chiun repeated himself, this time in Hebrew.

As Zhava turned to Remo, the morning sky darkened.

"Looks like rain," said Remo, "we had better put the jeep's top up."

Zhava continued to look at Remo even as they moved toward the car. Her eyes continued trying to pierce through his as they clipped on the canvas jeep top.

Remo thought he saw something in the back of her eyes, but then he remembered what Chiun had once said. "The eyes are not the windows of the soul. They mislead. The true window is the stomach. There, all life begins and ends. Look to the stomach, Remo."

Remo looked at Zhava's stomach. Her muscles were rippling under her shirt just enough for

118

Remo's trained eye to see them. To him, her stomach was jerking in and out like a piece of rice paper trying to control a pulsating flood.

Just as they finished securing the jeep top, large drops of rain started to fall.

"The storm is coming from the south," said Zhava. "Let us drive in that direction."

Remo started the engine and Zhava rode beside him. They passed through the rain. They passed through towns, and they passed kibbutzim. They passed children who played in bomb-made lakes. And they passed rusted Russian tanks with faded Egyptian markings.

Zhava began to talk. "My people, the ones I work for, do not think there is any conspiracy against the security of any weapons we may or may not have, no matter what *Time* magazine says. They can discover no connections among any of the murdered men. They think it is just a mad killer and, as such, simple police business."

"What do you think?" Remo asked.

"I think they are wrong," Zhava replied slowly. "I feel a danger all around us. I feel a noose around our necks." She was quiet for a moment, then continued briskly. "But my people do not work from feelings. They want to meet with you and see what you think."

"Naah," said Remo. "I don't like to meet new people. I'm not a good mixer."

"On my urging," said Zhava. "I think you are really here to help. Remo, I am not an agent for Israeli intelligence or the military."

"No kidding."

"I am an agent for the Zeher Lahurban."

"What's that?"

119

"The nuclear security agency. It means 'Remember the Destruction of the Temple.' The Jewish people's first two temples were destroyed long ago, leaving an entire race with no home. To us, Israel is the last temple."

Remo pulled over to the side of the road and stopped.

"Ooh," exclaimed Zhava. "Look, Remo. The flowers have bloomed from the rain."

As if by magic, flowers had appeared across the desert sands, creating an aromatic carpet of red, yellow, white, and blue. Zhava hopped out of the jeep and started walking through them. Remo followed. The landscape rivaled any garden Chiun could name. Remo walked alongside Zhava, their sides brushing.

She felt the flowers pet her ankles and the post-rain wind caress her face. "When I lost my fiancé," she said, "I thought that I would never feel again. I thought that I never could be happy. That life was only worth living if I worked to protect others from the same tragedy."

Zhava's words came slowly and carefully, as she tried to translate her Hebrew feelings into English. "Remo, I saw something in you that frightened me. I know we work in the same business, and I know you feel the same way I do. That the only thing that keeps up alive is our work."

"Now, wait . . ." said Remo.

"No, let me finish. I know you cannot help it anymore than I can. But now I see that your hopelessness, your emptiness, is wrong. It is wrong to deny happiness. It is wrong to deny hope."

Remo looked into Zhava's eyes and knew they were not misleading. He looked into her eyes and saw himself. He saw himself as he was years ago before Chiun's training had taken effect. When he thought the killing had some purpose, besides display of killing technique. So long ago.

Remo saw another girl in Zhava's eyes. Another girl with a job. Another girl that was everything that Zhava was. Good, brave, dedicated, soft, tough, honest, kind, and beautiful. A woman Remo had loved.

Her name had been Deborah, and she had been an Israeli agent, trained to hunt down Nazi war criminals. She had tracked Dr. Hans Frichtmann, butcher of Treblinka, to a think tank in Virginia. And there she met Remo.

They had one hour together before Frichtmann jammed enough heroin up her arm to wipe out an Army. Remo had paid the butcher in kind, but nothing could bring Deborah back. Not Remo, not Chiun, not CURE with all its computers, not even Zhava.

"Remo," Zhava's voice said from among the flowers. "Make me feel. I could be happy again if only I could feel."

Remo drifted in the flowers and felt like the Wizard of Oz. What did the tinman want? A heart. What did Zhava want? To feel. The tinman got a watch that ticked. What could he give Zhava?

Remo looked across the flowers that blanketed the desert. One part of him said that they would burn into straw in a few days. Another part of him said that that was no reason to deny their

121

beauty today. Remo took Zhava's hand and sat her down in the desert.

"I once got a letter," he said. "Who I got it from and why is unimportant now. Did you ever have a sister?"

Zhava shook her head no, tears forming in her eyes. Remo sat down next to her. "Anyway, I got this letter and it said, 'All of us carry our histories like crosses and our destinies like fools. But occasionally we must succumb to logic. And the logic of the situation is that our love would destroy us. If we could only shake our duties off like old dust. But we cannot.'"

Remo leaned back, sinking into the flowers, surprised that the letter came back into his mind word for word. He was happy he still remembered.

"'We gave each other an hour and a promise. Let us cherish that hour in the small places that keep us kind. Do not let your enemies destroy that. For as surely as the Jordan flows, we shall, if we maintain our goodness, meet again in the morning that never ends. This is our promise that we will keep.'"

Remo found his voice was shaking. He stopped talking and tried to swallow. But his throat was too dry. Why didn't Chiun's training cover voice shaking and throat dryness? Remo blinked and saw the gentle face of Zhava Fifer fill the sky. Her mouth was soft and smiling. Her eyes were not empty. Remo was not sure what they were filled with, but they were not empty.

"I only got my hour," he said.

122

Zhava came to him and whispered, "I will keep the promise."

Remo pulled her down and brought her shamma.

CHAPTER ELEVEN

CHAPTER ELEVEN

Irving Oded Markowitz slapped his stomach.
Then he slapped his forearms. Then he slapped
his thighs. Once he had assured himself that his
blood was flowing briskly, he punched the cellar
wall. Once with his right fist and once with his
left. Then he kicked the cellar wall with his bare
feet, first the right, then the left. Then he ran
around the room fifty times. Then he fell on his
face and did fifty push-ups. On the last one, he
threw his feet out in front of him, lay on his
back, and did fifty sit-ups. Then he stood and
slapped his stomach again.

He was ready, he thought.

Irving walked over to his rusted old gym
locker that he had ripped out of a merchant ship,
the U.S.S. *Crawlspace,* on which he had sailed
into the Haifa port fifteen years ago.

He pulled the door open and started to dress
while eyeing the pictures he had cut out of the

125

Israeli fashion magazines that lined the inside of the locker. All the pretty young Israeli models had their eyes and crotches blacked out by Markowitz with a thick-line felt-tipped pen.

Irving slid the white shirt on across his wide shoulders, then brought up the beige pants over his tightly muscled legs. While tying his tan tie, he kicked the wall a few more times. Then he slid on his shoulder holster with its heavy, silenced Italian eight-shot pistol. He slipped his beige jacket over that, then trotted upstairs.

"That you, Irving?" a shrill voice called in Hebrew from the kitchen.

"Yeah, Ma," said Irving. He plopped down into the brown stuffed sofa in front of the four heating pipes and pulled his worn tennis shoes out from underneath. He worked them onto his feet, rose, and walked over to the hallway mirror.

"What do you want for lunch?" came the shrill voice from the kitchen.

Irving checked his classic Jewish features to see if they were alright. "Nothing, Ma, I won't be in for lunch." The broken nose, care of Sigfried Gruber back in 1944, during stormtrooper training. Fine.

"No lunch?" said the voice from the kitchen. "You'll starve!"

The curly hair, care of Remington's styling kit, a Super Max drier, and a semi-annual permanent. Good.

"No, Ma, I won't. I'll pick up something."

A weak, sloping chin and brown eyes, care of plastic surgery and contact lenses. Excellent.

"What is it, Irving?" the voice from the kitchen inquired, then answered herself. "I know. You've found a nice girl and you're going out to lunch. Why don't you ever bring your friends home to lunch, Irving?"

Irving moved away from the mirror and gave his mother the finger through the living room wall.

"Ma, it's not a girl. I've just got to do some work."

"Oh," the voice from the kitchen sounded disappointed. "Is it for the nice man who works for the government?"

"Yes, Ma," said Irving Oded Markowitz. "For the nice man who works for the government." He walked through the dining room to the back door.

"Will you be home for dinner?" asked the voice from the kitchen.

"Yes, Ma," said Irving, then left. He walked down the back steps, across the small garden in the Markowitz's tiny backyard, and out the back gate into the alleyway.

As he reached the street, he felt like screaming for joy. Finally, after thirty years, action. Thirty years of training, thirty years of exercise, thirty years of hate, and finally, he, the man who had killed Irving Oded Markowitz with his bare hands, he, the man who had been Helmut Dorfmann, colonel in the Hitler Youth Corps, was finally called on by the Fatherland.

His mouth was wet in anticipation. His orders had been clear. The source had been impeccable. Straight from the top. He had gotten the word. It was only the two of them now. The rest had tried to run or had weakened. Now it was just he and

127

Horst. They would complete the job Hitler had begun.

At first, after the war, nothing had happened. He had drifted from place to place, keeping checks on the growth of the Jewish state and keeping himself in shape. Then, slowly, ever so slowly, he became part of the American Jewish movement. Meetings in Massachusetts, lobbying in Washington, moratoriums in New York. Infiltrating, growing with the ever blossoming Israel, helping it to get enough rope to strangle itself.

Dorfmann had only to follow orders and drop an occasional note to his "parents." But then the word came. Ingratiate and infiltrate. So Dorfmann had become the man he had killed, and the Markowitz's "son," reported missing in action, finally came home to the Holy Land to stay.

Dorfmann had helped at his "father's" watchshop and gone shopping for his "mother." For long, hateful years, he nurtured their blindness, ate their food, and had only black death in his heart.

But now his time had come. Soon the Markowitzes would be no more. All he had to do was kill two men. Just kill two men and his "father's" cloying face would disappear. His "mother's" sopping attention would vanish, and maybe then his nightmares with Irving's face would cease.

Just two men and he could return to Germany, let his hair grow out, change his face, and read of Israel's destruction.

Just two men. Two American agents. What were their names again? Oh, yes, Remo and Chiun. Regarded as highly dangerous.

128

Irving Oded Markowitz felt the heat of the heavy automatic against his ribs. He could almost hear the pistol's heartbeat. It hummed, it shone, it buzzed. Soon now, he promised it, soon.

Irving walked along Ben Yehuda feeling the early afternoon heat. He reveled in his sweat, only wishing it to grow hotter and hotter and hotter still until the flesh blackened and the buildings crumbled and the Jews turned on each other like mad dogs. What a joke. A thirty-year joke that would never die.

Irving walked into the Israel Sheraton, whistling, his hands in his pockets. His mind was uncluttered by strategy as he stepped into a waiting elevator and pushed a button for the eighth floor.

He would simply wait until the time was right, break open the door, and shoot them both. No television solutions. No gas through the ventilator shaft, no acid through the shower head.

Just two pieces of lead traveling through pasty bone at just under the speed of sound. Bang, bang. Simple.

Irving Oded Markowitz stepped out of the elevator onto the eighth floor and walked to the door of the suite he was told the Americans would be in. He looked both ways, then listened. He heard a conversation in Hebrew, so someone must be inside.

He hit the door with his right shoulder.

There was a small cracking sound as the door bolt was ripped clean out of the frame, popping across the room and onto a bed.

Irving moved into the suite low and fast, pulling out his sleek, dark blue, Italian pistol. He was two steps in as his mind registered the sitting figure not ten feet away. The thirty years of exercise and muscle development had been waiting for this very moment. Even as Irving's eyes were taking in the pale yellow kimono that nestled around the sitting figure, his hand snapped in front of him. Even as his mind registered the sparse wisps of white hair atop the sitting figure's head, the gun barrel was pointed and Irving's finger tightened twice.

The soft coughs of the silenced revolver were wrapped in the heavy suite's carpeting and curtains. Those sounds died as the color television set across the room crackled and spit sparks. Two spider-web holes were visible in the darkened screen.

A high-pitched Oriental voice said calmly, "You may tell Emperor Smith it is not necessary for him to destroy the previous set upon delivery of a new one. I can take care of that myself."

Irving straightened as the final frustrated sputter died from the TV set. Sitting on the bed, fingering the door bolt, was a small wizened Oriental.

"It was an arithmetic program," the Oriental said. "Tell the emperor that his prompt delivery has been much appreciated and his wisdom is all encompassing. Now, please, my daytime dramas?"

Markowitz snapped his weapon into a clean line with his eye so that the pistol's sights seemed to be holding up the Chinaman's nose. Get hold of yourself, Helmut, he told himself, shooting at figures on a television screen is not good. Remember, technique is the key.

His finger tightened on the trigger once more.

He heard the soft cough and felt the warm kick of the recoil. It was a fine shot. Smooth, clean, technically perfect. What the Chink was doing in the Americans' apartment, and whatever he was asking for, Markowitz would never know. Because the bullet would soon spread his yellow brains all over the wall.

"I suppose this means that you are not the American messenger and are merely more of the amateur help that abounds in this land of little beauty," said an Oriental voice in his ear.

Irving stared in wonder at the smoking hole in the backboard of the bed, then turned to see the Oriental at the room's writing desk.

He spun toward the small man, crying, "What trick is this, swine?" His gun centered itself on the Oriental's stomach. Messenger? Amateur help? Beauty? He thought, Do not let this clutter your mind. You are Helmut Dorfmann, finest shot in your class. Think of the stimulus, direct the bullet with your mind, then fire.

Irving's trigger finger tightened thrice more. The mirror above the writing desk cracked, and the bureau's formica top shattered. The Oriental sat in the lotus position in an armchair across the room. "One cannot trust Americans for anything," he said. "Not even a simple delivery. I await beauty. Instead, I get a creature with pieces of plastic in his eyes, blond roots in his hair, and scars of surgery around his neck, and a gun in his hand. Why do you hate the furniture of my room? Because if it is simply ugliness you punish, you will need a bigger gun."

Markowitz's mind reeled. How could the Chinaman have known about the surgery? The hair dye? The contact lenses? Was it all a trap? His gun sought out the Oriental's heart as if by its own will. He cried out: "For the German people, die. Die." The gun jerked twice in his hands. Irving squeezed his eyes shut, then pried them open again.

The Oriental was standing directly before him, shaking his head. "Not for the German people," he said. "Oh, no. They hired this house once for a mission, and they did not pay. Would you like to hear about it?"

Markowitz stood dumbly in the center of the room. His eyes flitted over the damage to the bed, the shattered television, the writing desk. The back of the reading chair was torn into little pieces. Small bits of stuffing still floated down to the carpet. Chips of wood had smashed a lamp and wedged themselves into a closet. But the Oriental stood unharmed before him.

Markowitz cried in rage, gripped his gun in both hands, pushed the barrel into the Oriental's face and fired. The hammer clicked on an empty chamber.

"I will tell you," said the Oriental from behind Markowitz. "They asked me to solve a problem concerning the little man with the little mustache. He heard I was coming. He was so frightened he killed even a woman."

Markowitz blinked. He looked down at the barrel of his revolver. It was straight. Perhaps his food had been poisoned.

"And then they refused to pay us," the old Oriental said. "It was not our fault he killed himself, this little fool. Did you know he ate carpeting?"

132

Too much. First to make a fool of the son of the Reich and then to insult the Fuehrer himself. Too much. The man must die.

"Demon," cried the man who had been Helmut Dorfmann. "I must kill you with my own two hands."

His hands stretched across the space between them, his fingers claws, toughened by his years on the sea, by his daily exercise, to rip out the cursed yellow throat from which poured the evil lies about Hitler.

But before his fingers could grip, there was a blur passing before his eyes. Suddenly, he did not seem to have hands to kill with.

His charge stopped, and he brought up his arms. Mounds of red were sliding down his jacket and his throat constricted into a horrible, choking sound. He found his feet, but before he could run, there was another blur, and the blur seemed to encircle him, and there were two small tugs at his shoulders.

Irving's numbed shock turned into bursting pain and his mouth opened and his eyes squeezed shut. He felt as if he were floating and his legs were gone. Then he thought he felt the thick hotel carpeting on his back. Then there was only the incredible pain. Then nothing.

Chiun decided to wait in the lobby for his shipment of video tapes. Hopefully Remo would be back soon to clean up the mess.

133

CHAPTER TWELVE

"Remo," said Zhava, "this is Yoel Zabari, the head of the Zeher Lahurban, and Tochala Delit, my immediate superior. Gentleman, this is Remo Williams."

"Mr. Weel-yums," said Yoel Zabari.

"Mr. Zahoring, Mr. Delish," said Remo.

"Zabari, Delit," said Zhava.

"Gotcha," Remo said.

They stood in the third-floor office of the nuclear security agency, after a three and a half hour drive that did almost nothing to diminish the aroma of the desert flowers that clung to them.

Two more comfortable-looking red padded chairs had been added to the office, one facing Zabari's desk, the other across from where Delit sat.

Now the two of them moved into the room as the male Israelis sat. Zhava, still somewhat flushed, her skin clinging to a never before experienced creamy tone, strode to the chair by Zabari's side. Delit sat across from her.

"Please sit down," said Zabari in heavily accented English. "Zhava, you are looking well. Mr. Williams, it is with great pleasure that we meet."

Remo saw that this was what the man's half-a-mouth said. The look in his one good eye and the way he sat said, "It is a pleasure to have someone as dangerous as yourself in a position where I can kill you if necessary."

Remo sat in the chair across from him. "You got banged up pretty bad. A bomb? And it's no pleasure being here. What kind of a country are you people running anyway?"

Zhava sucked in her breath and her flush blushed, turning her the shade of tomato soup. Zabari, however, replied easily.

"So this is the famous American bluntness, eh? Surely, Mr. Williams, we cannot be to blame for your problems. 'Tourists' must be careful when they walk the desert at night. As the Talmud says, 'A human being is here today, in the grave tomorrow.'" The left side of his face smiled.

The right side of Remo's face smirked back. "The Book of Sinanju says, 'I have lived fifty years to know the mistakes of forty-nine.'"

"Ah," said Yoel Zabari, looking pleased, "but the Talmud also states, 'The Lord hates him who talks one way and thinks another.'"

"The Book of Sinanju replies, 'We sleep with legs outstretched, free of true, free of false.'"

"I see," Zabari mused. "The Wisdom of the Talmud includes, however, 'One who commits a crime as an agent, is also a criminal.'"

135

"How true," said Remo cordially. "Sinanju says, 'The perfect man leaves no trace of his conduct.' "

"Hmmm," said Zabari, considering, then quoted, " 'Worry kills the strongest man.' "

Remo replied in Chiun's sing-song, " 'Training is not knowledge and knowledge is not strength. But combine knowledge with training and one will get strength.' Or at least I think that's how it goes."

Zabari cocked his one good eye at Remo and leaned forward in his chair.

" 'Loose talk leads to sin,' " he said, then as an afterthought, adding the Talmudic source, "Abot."

" 'Think twice, then say nothing,' " Remo replied. "Chiun."

Delit and Fifer still sat on either side of the desk, between the two combatants, their heads moving back and forth, as if watching a tennis game.

It was Zabari's serve.

" 'Even a thief prays that he will succeed.' "

Remo returned, " 'Never cut a man with words. They become a weapon against you.' "

Delit's and Fifer's heads turned to Zabari.

" 'Silence is good for the learned. All the more for fools.' "

Back to Remo.

" 'Learn to cut a man with your eyes. They are sometimes stronger than your hands.' "

Zabari: " 'A man is born with closed hands; he expects to grab the whole world. He dies with open hands; he takes nothing with him.' "

136

Remo: " 'Everything is a weapon in the hands of a man who understands.' "

Match point.

Zabari burst out laughing, slapping the desk with an open palm. "By God," he cried, turning to Fifer, "he is one of us."

Zhava smiled warmly.

"I'm glad you're happy," said Remo. "All I had left was, 'Spring comes and the grass grows.' "

Zabari laughed harder. "I will tell you the truth," he finally managed. "All I had left was, 'A man should teach his child a profession—also how to swim!' "

Remo and Zhava joined in the laughter until Delit coughed softly.

"Of course," said Zabari, calming. "Sorry, Toe, but you know how much I love the Talmud." Still, Zabari could not hide a left-sided grin as he turned to Remo. "Now, Mr. Williams . . ."

"Remo."

"Very well, Remo. We have checked and double-checked," Zabari said, "but we can find no evidence of your standing as an American agent."

Remo wanted to ask how they had found out he was an agent in the first place, but instead he said, "I'd say that ought to be proof enough."

Zabari looked at Delit, who nodded. "A fair appraisal," Zabari conceded, "since everywhere you go there follows damage and destruction to both sides of the conflict. Besides the extermination of four terrorists . . ."—Zabari took a moment to spit in the wastepaper basket— ". . . there was a blast at an Israeli sulphur plant not far away.

Our agent Fifer reported you were in the area. We could not overlook that coincidence."

Zhava looked as if she wished they had.

"I can't help it if I'm unlucky," said Remo. "But I thought the idea of this meeting was to share opinions, not cross-examine my references."

"True," said Zabari, his left profile darkening. "We can find no connection between any of these terrorists and the Israelis that were so brutally mutilated. True, Toe?"

Tochala Delit ran his hand through his dark hair while checking the latest reports on his lap. "True," he said finally.

"Mr. Will ... uh, Remo, have your people uncovered a connection?"

Remo looked at their faces. There was an electric silence in the room for a moment, then he replied, "No."

Zhava's face did not change. Zabari leaned back in his chair. Delit sighed.

"Then, what do you think is going on?" asked Zabari.

"You got me," said Remo. "As far as I know, the Arabs are trying to acquire a chicken soup monopoly. My people have come up with zilch."

"There it is then," interrupted Delit, "It is as I said it was, Yoel. Israel is overrun with foreign agents. There is no connection between these mutilations, the attempts on Remo, and the security this office is responsible for."

"I tend to agree, Toe," said Zabari, then directed himself back to the American. "These men who have been trying to kill you probably see you as just another American spy to be gotten rid of. It has nothing to do with our agency or our ... uh,

138

project." Even though everyone in the office knew what they were talking about, no one could seem to bring himself to say it.

Tochala Delit checked the time on his extra-width Speidel twist-a-flex wristwatch, then motioned a high sign to Zabari.

"Oh, yes, Toe, quite right. You must excuse us. It is the Yom Hazikaron today." He saw the question on Remo's face, then explained, "Our Remembrance Day. I am afraid we must call this meeting to a close since Mr. Delit and myself have many obligations to fulfill."

Zabari and Delit rose. Zhava got up to show Remo the way out.

"However," Zabari continued, "I do suggest that you consider another line of work since your cover is so completely blown. Say, continued study of this book of See-nan-you. It would be of great sorrow to me if you were to meet your ancestors in Israel."

Remo rose, raising his eyebrows. Was that a thinly disguised threat?

"Don't worry about me," he told Zabari. "As the Book of Sinanju says, 'Fear not death and it cannot become your enemy.'"

Zabari was shaking his head sadly as Zhava showed Remo out.

CHAPTER THIRTEEN

The service, as always, was in the evening, the eve of Yom Ha'atsmaut, the Israeli Independence Day. It always fell on the fifth day of Iyar on the Hebrew calendar, but it is different each year on Western calendars.

It is also different from the West in many other important ways. There are no celebrations, no fireworks, no barbecues. There is no poetry, and little sermonizing. There is only the continuing agonizing awareness of reality, the tortured memories of past persecution, and the firm conviction that the massacres, the pogroms, the holocaust must-never-happen-again.

They honored the dead for one night, then went back to war the following morning.

Zhava explained this to Remo before she too had to leave in order to pay tribute to her family and traditions. She gave Remo her telephone number, at her grandmother's in case he wanted to reach her, then left. As Remo ambled back to the hotel, Tochala Delit and Yoel Zabari marched in a somber military parade up the Avenue of the Righteous Gentiles.

They marched up the ridge called Har Hazikaron, the Hill of the Remembrance, then stopped before a rectangular building made of uncut boulders and jagged, twisted steel. The Yad Vashem Memorial.

The Israeli military fired salutes, British style. A confused little girl, who was too young to remember, or even comprehend what she was doing here, ignited the Memorial Flame. Then the kaddish was recited. The Prayer for the Dead.

Some in the crowd remembered how it had been. Some hated. Some cried at the memory of murdered loved ones. One man was swelled with pride.

This man knew that without him, and others like him, they would not be standing before this nightmarish memorial. Without him and those like him, no hill could have been dedicated to the six million dead. Without him, there would be no fears, no hate. This was his monument. This was the memorial to a nation of Nazis.

The man who had been Horst Vessel slipped away from the crowd as a government official began a speech. He wandered inside the Yad Vashem to see again what he had helped do and to commune with his past.

It would be all right. No one would notice him gone. Not Zhava Fifer, too pious, too dedicated to her cause to lift her head up from prayer. Not the incredibly stupid Yoel Zabari, who was even

142

now listening to the piteous platitudes that rolled over the crowd of sullen fools.

No one would notice if Tochala Delit slipped away.

Tochala Delit stepped into the crypt-like inner room of the memorial. He stood proudly in the huge stone room, the lone, naked flame in the middle sending an eerie burning light flickering across his high cheekbones and dark hair.

The muscles in his thick wrists clenched and unclenched as he slid his heels across the floor, across the plaques that recorded the Nazi death camps of World War II. Across Bergen-Belsen, across Auschwitz, across Dachau, until Tochala Delit came to his own. Treblinka. His personal holocaust. The man who had been Horst Vessel remembered, trembling with pride.

It had been his idea. They were losing the war. It was not traitorous to admit that. Not if he had a plan to use that very fact against the enemy. The only true enemy. The Jews. The others were only fighting for their misdirected ideals. They would soon come around. But the Jews, who embodied those misdirected ideals, they would have to be dealt with.

Tochala Delit heard words being chanted from outside. He dimly recognized them as the prophet Maimonides' thirteen articles of Faith. He heard the words that were chanted every morning by many Israelis and translated them.

"God is our only Leader."

Hitler is mine, thought Delit.

"God is One."

It is only a matter of time.

"God has no body."

Soon, neither will any of you.

"God is first and last."

The last part of that is true.

"We should pray to Him only."

See if that will help.

"The words of the Prophets are true, the prophecies of Moses are true."

Soon you can ask them yourselves.

"The Torah was given through God to Moses. The Torah will never be changed."

Not changed. Destroyed.

"God knows the thoughts of all. God rewards good deeds and punishes evil."

Then God must feel I'm right.

"We shall await the coming of the Messiah."

You do not have long to wait.

"We believe in the Resurrection of the Dead."

You had better.

Tochala Delit felt very good. On this, the last day of the last Jewish temple, he remembered it all. How he had trained a specially selected group of Nazis. Fritz Barber, who had become Moishe Gavan. Helmut Dorfmann, who had become Irving Markowitz. Joseph Brunhein, who became Ephraim Hegez. And Leonard Essendorf who had become Ben Isaac Goldman. He remembered how they had starved themselves to join the ranks at the concentration camp, Treblinka. How they had all circumcised themselves as a sign of faith. How they all became Jewish in the closing days of World War II. How they had all infiltrated the Jewish state with their specialized talents and how they were all united in the fervent dream of destruction.

144

Tochala Delit listened to the voices from outside, declaring their national anthem, "Hatikva."

> "So long as still within our breasts
> The Jewish heart beats true.
> So long as still toward the East
> To Zion looks the Jew.
> So long as hopes are not yet lost
> Two thousand years we cherished them
> To live in freedom in the land
> Of Zion and Jerusalem."

But that was not what Horst Vessel heard. Swaying in a near hallucinatory state, he heard:

> "So long as it is still within your breasts
> The Jewish end is due.
> So long as Hitler towers o'er the rest
> To destruction is the Jew.
> You think your hope is not yet lost
> In this, stupid people, you are wrong.
> You will die here from your own bombs.
> So long, Jewish swine, so long."

Tochala Delit reached under his pale jacket to his inside pocket. As the echoes died away, he pulled out a small rectangular black box with wiring coming from it. It looked like a metal tarantula lying in his palm.

He was ready. The ones who weakened had been destroyed. They had been cast away in a manner befitting their treachery. Ripped into the swastika shape.

But now the dead did not matter. The millions of Jews did not matter. The two Americans did not matter. The tiny black box would send them all into space where the ghost of Hitler awaited.

The Fourth Reich was about to begin. The heavenly Reich.

From outside the abstract pattern of anguished, agonized steel that made up the Yad Vashem doors came trembling voices singing "Ani Ma'amin." Zhava Fifer, Yoel Zabari, and all the others gathered there sang it. It expressed their faith in God even during their darkest moments. It had often been sung by Jews on their way to the Nazi gas chambers and ovens.

Tochala Delit slipped the box back into his jacket and left the room still glowing with pride.

After all, they were singing his song.

CHAPTER FOURTEEN

"Is that your idea of a joke?" Remo said in the middle of the Israel Sheraton lobby. "A body in the middle of the living room? Not even a towel dropped anywhere to soak up the blood?"

Chiun sat with his back to Remo, lost in the passing of air across his face.

"I am getting sick and tired of this stuff," Remo said. "You are inconsiderate. As well as petty."

Chiun began to study the intricate pattern of the lobby carpet.

"I won't go away," said Remo, "just because you're impersonating a wall."

Remo stared at the back of Chiun's neck.

"Answer me."

Silence.

"All right, then," Remo said, "I'm going to sit here until you do."

"Good," Chiun said suddenly, "We can wait for

147

my tapes together. What is this that you interrupt my meditative leisures? Are you speaking of your mess upstairs?"

"My mess? My mess? How can you call that up there my mess?"

"No doubt that the mess was looking for you, since I am only of secondary importance. Why should any mess seek out one as petty and inconsiderate as my simple self?"

Remo felt the inevitable grip on him as surely as a hand around his throat. He decided to surrender by silence.

Chiun would not have it. "You know what you have not done?"

"What?"

"You have not sent the Norman Lear, Norman Lear message."

"If I send the letter, you will clean up the mess?" he asked.

"If you send it, I will allow you to clean it up."

"And if I do not send it?" Remo asked.

"Then you will need something else to occupy your time. Cleaning will keep your mind from mischief."

Remo threw his hands into the air in disgust. Then the ringing voice of Schlomo Artov burst into his ear.

"Aha," it cried. "At it again, eh? I warned you about abusing your father, young man. What is the matter with you?"

"Yes," Chiun echoed. "What is the matter with you?"

"Keep out of this," Remo growled to Artov.

"I heard the whole thing," Artov said. "Imag-

148

ine, yelling at your father." He turned to Chiun. "Mr. Lear, you have my sympathy."

"Mr. Who?" said Chiun.

"And you, Norman," Artov told Remo. "For shame."

"Who is this lunatic?" Chiun asked Remo.

"Ignore him," Remo said. "He's just another man about to have an asthma attack."

"Nonsense," said Artov. "I never felt better in my . . . agha-woosh." Artov suddenly got the worst asthma attack in his aghawoosh. He leaned over in breathless pain and allowed Remo to escort him back to his desk. Remo assured him that he would be feeling better soon, then took his protective hand from deep inside the bones of Schlomo's right shoulder. He sat the poor reservations man down, and soon Artov did feel better even though his full speaking voice would not return for two weeks.

Remo walked back to Chiun.

"Why don't we just mosey upstairs," Remo said pleasantly through clenched teeth, "where we can talk without disturbing anyone else."

"I like it here. I am waiting for my daytime dramas," said Chiun.

"Smith might be trying to call," said Remo.

"Let him. I have dealt with enough lunatics in one day."

"I will never mail that letter," Remo said.

"Very will," begrudged Chiun. "I suppose I must supervise your cleaning. I can never trust you to do anything right yourself."

Remo stopped off at the gift shop to buy some luggage and string before they arrived back at

149

their bloody suite. As Remo was cramming Irving Oded Markowitz in, the phone rang.

"Janitorial service," Remo said. "You kill 'em, I clean 'em."

The silence on the other end was like a look into a black cave.

"It's incredible, Smitty," said Remo. "Even your silence is sour."

"If I had never seen you," said Harold W. Smith, "I would not believe you could exist."

"What have you got, Smitty? I'm pretty busy." Remo cracked the right knee of the corpse to fit him into the bag.

"Maybe nothing, maybe everything," said Smith, "The men who ... er, greeted you on arrival came through the concentration camp Treblinka during World War II."

"So?"

"The murdered industrialist, Hegez, and Goldman, were also in Treblinka."

"Oh?"

"And Dr. Moishe Gavan."

"All of them? Same place? Are you sure?" Remo asked.

"Yes," said Smith. He sat in Rye, New York, looking at the sole outlet to a network of computer systems whose size, range, and scope made the IBM warehouse look like an erector set. This small outlet on his desk enabled him to tap the resources of millions of people, thousands of businesses, schools, libraries, and churches, hundreds of nooks and a good many crannies.

But it was up to Smith to take the reams of fossilized information and see what it meant in terms of the nation and the world. Usually his desk was covered with a fair amount of this information, but now the only thing there was a typewritten, four-page list he had discovered because a woman's sister, who belonged to the American Jewish Committee, which combats anti-Semitism, and B'nai Brith, a fraternal order, had a daughter who met a man through B'nai Akiba, a religious youth organization, whom she married, and they had a son who was counseled as he grew older by the U.S. Jewish Board of Guardians, which specializes in child guidance, which led to the boy joining the YMHA, the Young Men's Hebrew Association, which provides cultural activities to Jewish youth, where his first endeavor was to contribute a report on oppression in World War II, complete with concentration-camp lists, which so impressed his counselor that he sent it to the United Synagogue, a union of American temples, which entered it into their bank of computerized microfilm, where it happened to cross Smith's desk and the head of CURE saw a connection. A slim, impossible connection. The kind CURE specialized in.

"I'm very sure," said Smith. "Why?"

"Hold on a minute," said Remo. He opened the suitcase, which he had just stood on to close. He ignored the bulging blue eyes that popped out of the purple face, instead reaching down across the body's torso and plucking something out of its blood-soaked jacket. He closed the suitcase again and tried to open the small billfold.

"Just a second," he called down to the receiver. "The blood is all sticky." He found what he was looking for and picked up the phone.

"How about an Irving Oded Markowitz?" he asked.

"Just a second," said Smith.

Remo hummed as Chiun appeared in the room, as if by magic.

"Yes," said Smith, "Markowitz was at Treblinka too. How did you know?"

"He came to visit Chiun. I'll get back to you."

Remo hung up. He felt a surge of self-discovery like a mental connection and an electric belt buckling. A swirling wind coursed through his body, clearing out the cobwebs. Now he knew how Sherlock Holmes felt when he discovered the truth of a crime. Detective work could be fun.

"You look sick," said Chiun. "Did Smith say my daytime dramas were delayed?"

"Relax, Little Father," Remo said happily, dialing another number. "They'll arrive tomorrow, after the Jewish holiday."

"A day without drama . . ." said Chiun.

"Is like a morning without orange juice," finished Remo, phone to his ear. "Hello? May I speak to Zhava please? What? Huh? Speak English, please. Zhava! No speak-a de lan-guage. Bagel! Come on, get-me-Zha-va!"

Chiun took the phone from Remo's hand. "Must I do everything?" he inquired of the ceiling. Then he held a conversation in fluent old world Hebrew with the woman on the other end.

After what seemed like a half-hour, he handed the phone back to Remo. "She is getting the young lady. Ask Zhava why she never writes."

"What were you two talking about?" asked Remo, phone to his ear again.

152

"The universal problem of all good people," Chiun replied. "The ingratitude of our children."

"Keep telling yourself that," Remo said, as Zhava came on the line.

"Remo, already? You pick the worst times."

"Well, this is important," Remo said, then told her the information Smith had related.

"But Tochala Delit said he found no connections between the men," Zhava said when Remo had finished.

"Zhava, where was Delish during the war?"

"Which one?"

"World War II."

"Everyone know that. He went through torture in . . . Oh, my God! Treblinka."

Remo took that in, savoring his following words. "I thought so."

"I was right then," said Zhava. "There is something going on."

"And what better day than your Fourth of July or whatever you call it?"

"We must learn what this means. Remo, meet me at Delit's house, right away." She gave him an address and hung up.

"You have that same sickly look as before," said Chiun. "It must be the water."

But Remo would not let Chiun dampen his joy. "The game is afoot, Watson," he said. "Want to come?"

"Who is Watson?" Chiun asked.

153

CHAPTER FIFTEEN

Tochala Delit had a small home on the outskirts of Tel Aviv. It was a simple affair of sand-blasted brick with a large library, a comfortable living room, a small bedroom, a cozy tile porch, and a wet bathroom.

When Zhava Fifer drove up, Remo and Chiun were sitting on the front stoop reading a sheet of paper. Both looked relaxed except for some dirt that had accumulated on the bottom of Remo's tan slacks. Chiun wore a blood red kimono with black and gold highlights. Both men were barefoot.

"How did you get here so fast?" asked Zhava. "I was driving like a mad person all the way."

"We ran," said Remo simply. "We would have been here sooner. But Chiun wanted to change his clothes."

"I was not wearing a running kimono," Chiun

explained. "It is a small city, but still no reason to waste an opportunity."

Zhava got out of the jeep and ran over to them.

"Is he here? Where is Delit?" she asked.

"He's out," said Remo, not looking up from the white lined sheet of paper he held in his hand.

"What is that?" asked Zhava. "What have you found?"

"It is a poem," said Chiun.

"The bathroom is lined with them. But I think this one will interest you."

"I tried to have him give you a nicer one," said Chiun, "but he would not listen. His lack of taste is well known."

Zhava read aloud,

"As the khamsin roars in from the plain,
So too comes the glorious pain,
A blasting sun-like solar heat,
Covers the Jews with its shroud-like sheet.
Eyes will bake,
Feet will cake,
Heads will burst,
That is not the worst,
Cities will crumble,
The skies will rumble.
The ghost of Hitler is satisfied at last,
When the home of the Jews is in the past.
Look for the death across the sand,
The last independence day in Jewland."

"He is planning to detonate a nuclear bomb," Zhava cried.

"That's what I figured," said Remo.

"That is what you figured," scoffed Chiun. "Who had to read this poem to you?"

"I can't help it if I don't know Hebrew. Besides, you edited it. I don't remember anything about feet caking."

"I thought it ineffective," said Chiun. "I improved it."

" 'Vultures will mate' is an improvement?"

"Please, please," interrupted Zhava. "We cannot waste time. We still do not know where he is planning to detonate. We have installations in the Sinai, Galilee, Haifa . . ."

"Can I open a franchise?" asked Remo.

"This is not funny," screamed Zhava. "He is going to blow up Israel."

Remo rose quickly. "All right, going crazy won't do much good. Look, it says right in the poem something about khamsin and the death from the sand. The sand must be the desert, but what's khamsin?"

"Brilliant," said Chiun.

"Elementary," Remo replied.

"Khamsin are easterly winds that blow across the Negev," said Zhava. "He must be returning to the Sodom installation."

"I could have told you that," said Chiun.

Remo grimaced at Chiun, then talked quickly. "Zhava, you get Zaborich . . ."

"Zabari."

"And we'll meet you at the Dead Sea."

"All right," said Zhava leaping into her jeep. Remo watched her speed off.

"Hey, this detective stuff is easier than I thought," Remo said.

"Brilliant one," intoned Chiun from the stoop.

157

"Your wisdom is all-encompassing. Not only have you allowed the one method of four-wheel transportation to leave without us, but you stand about declaring your brilliance. To be elated at nothing is to lose hold on reality. How can such a one be truly a master of himself?"

Remo would not let Chiun dampen his pride. "Petty," he growled.

"If Petty were here," said Chiun, "it would not be necessary to cross the desert by foot."

"What the hell, Chiun," said Remo. "This way is faster."

He began to run.

Zhava burst into the Zabari home as Mrs. Zabari was lighting the Sabbath candles. Zhava was dusty and out of breath. As she staggered in, Yoel and his four children looked up from the table.

They had just finished dessert and the children's faces were flushed with satisfaction and pride. For their father's work today during the Remembrance services had been well received.

"What is it?" asked Yoel. "What is the matter?"

Zhava stared at the Sabbath candles. She remembered from her lessons as a child that the eight candles, lit every Friday, represented peace, freedom, and the light that radiates from the human soul.

Zhava's eyes turned to the children. Blond, dark-eyed Daphna, who would make a fine ballerina one day. Eight-year-old Dov, whose hope for peace touched everyone he met. Stephen, the athlete, the fighter, the believer in an ultimate

158

truth. And Melissa, stepping from childhood into being a woman. A whole woman in a world of fragmented femininity.

Zhava saw the looks on their faces and the innocence in their eyes, remembering why she had come here. She thought of what Tochala Delit was planning to do. It must not happen. She could not let it.

She felt the warm hand of Shula, Mrs. Zabari, on her arm, and saw the concerned face of Yoel Zabari.

"You must come," she said breathlessly. "It is important."

Zabari looked deep into her eyes. He turned to look at the Sabbath candles. He turned to his wife, who stood, asking silent questions. He turned to his children, who had already forgotten Zhava's entrance and were entertaining themselves at the table. Dov had put one spoon on top of another and now brought his hand down. One spoon served as a catapult and the other spoon flipped end over end until Dov caught it in mid-air. He smiled. Daphna applauded.

"Yes," said Yoel. "I will come. Now?"

Zhava nodded.

"Excuse me, my dear," he said, brushing his wife's cheek with the ravaged right side of his face. She smiled warmly. "Excuse me, children, I will be back soon," he said waving at the table.

"Aw, Dad, do you have to?" said Stephen.

Zabari nodded sadly, then looked up at the ceiling. "Excuse me, Lord." After all, it was the Sabbath.

Yoel Zabari went with Zhava.

"Are we going back to the labyrinth of pipes so that you can get lost again?" asked Chiun.

"Not this time," said Remo. "I'm rolling now."

They continued running. Remo's strides were long, even, and smooth, as if he were walking along a moving conveyor belt. Certainly not as if he were struggling across the sands of a desert. His arms moved easily at his sides, in rhythm with the drumming of his legs.

Chiun's hands, however, were deep in the sleeves of his red and black kimono, his skirt-like train billowing behind him. The hem always just touched the desert sand. He was arched slightly forward and slicing across the air like a thrown knife. He never seemed to move his legs because his kimono remained back in the wind, uninterrupted by any forward movement.

"Remo," Chiun said, "I would like to say that you have acted most wisely."

Remo stumbled. Struggling to regain his stride, he managed to speak. "Thank you, Little Father."

"Yes, my son," Chiun intoned, "training is not knowledge and knowledge is not strength, but combine training with knowledge and then you will have strength."

"Believe it or not, Chiun, I know that," Remo said.

The two continued across the deepening horizon.

"What I want to say, Remo, is that you are behaving as a Master should."

Remo was pleased. He stood straighter, his eyes took in the sky, and his stride grew wider and stronger. This was indeed his day.

160

"Thank you," he said. "I can't say how much . . ."

"Except," continued Chiun, "that you jump badly, you cannot drive, and you are insulting. You behave like a Master who is insulting and weak."

"You old faker," said Remo. "You set me up for that." Remo tried to race ahead, but Chiun matched his speed, foot for foot.

And his voice continued as clear as a desert breeze.

"You have not sent the Norman Lear, Norman Lear message. You begrudge a man his simple pleasures. You do not clean your mess. You are a litterbug. You . . ."

Remo and Chiun continued across the sand, side by side.

161

CHAPTER SIXTEEN

The first perimeter guard had been surprised when the car on the main access road to the Zeher Lahurban sulphur plant stopped and Tochala Delit himself poked his head out.

The second perimeter guard had been stunned, and the third astonished. They had all found it unusual that Tochala Delit himself should be in the car alone and that his clothing was so heavy on so hot a day, but if Tochala Delit himself found it necessary, then it must have been necessary.

And if Tochala Delit himself said that no one else should be allowed in, then no one else would be allowed in. And if Tochala Delit himself said not even the prime minister, then not even the prime minister. And if Tochala Delit himself instructed that these orders were to be followed implicitly, then the three guards would be pleased and honored to lay down their lives for those orders.

But Tochala Delit himself acted strangely today, didn't he?

Tochala Delit himself entered the heart of the nuclear installation through a simple metal door, which he locked behind him.

He stood in the low, metal-reinforced concrete hallway sloping deep down to the room with no exit. He patted his inside jacket pocket for the hundredth time that afternoon. The layers of clothing and the hard, thin box were still there, giving him strength.

Thirty years. Thirty years, and now the end was in sight. But thirty years was a long time. Tochala Delit was an old man now. The man who had been Horst Vessel thought about his life. He felt warm blood flow in his veins again. He saw the twisted bodies of the people he had killed in the name of purity. He heard their cries, their screams, their prayers, their ranting. And now, to end like this. Riding the tip of a nuclear-powered mushroom cloud. Because whatever the bomb did not destroy, the surviving Arabs would. Israel was doomed.

Horst Vessel filled his lungs with the stuffy air and felt the salty beads of excitement on his brow. At that moment he would not have changed places with anyone on earth.

Remo took the first perimeter fence like a hurdler. Chiun followed like a parachute toy that one puffs into the air and it floats to the ground.

"We have entered a different part of the field,"

164

Chiun said. "We now stand on explosive ground."

"Mine field," said Remo. "I was wondering why the ground seemed different."

"Good," said Chiun. "You remain wondering, and I will see you in the kingdom of Heaven. Be sure to greet my ancestors for me."

"Come on," said Remo. "We don't have much time."

"Let us go quickly then," said Chiun, "for if you walk as badly as you jump, we are both doomed."

They moved across the sand with the combined weight of a tablespoon of whipped cream.

Coming to the second perimeter, the infrared fence, Chiun motioned to Remo ahead.

"Let us see if you have learned anything," he said.

Remo hopped over as easily as if he were taking a step. Chiun followed suit.

"Wonderful," said Chiun, "you now rank with the grasshopper, which jumps well."

"I'm sorry I opened my mouth," Remo said.

"So am I," said Chiun.

Since the area was barren and neither of them had tripped an alarm, their paths were uncrossed by blazing lead or flaming missiles. They easily transversed the third perimeter, and soon Remo and Chiun stood among the spiraling machinery of the sulphur plant.

"So here we are," said Remo. "See any atomic bombs laying around?"

Chiun stood implacable, looking like an ancient cog in a giant machine.

Remo leaned against a bolted metal door and

felt vibrations emanating from its other side. Part of the sulphur machinery, he thought.

"Since this is still the outskirts of the plant," he said, "I guess we can figure the nuclear area is closer to the middle. A couple of miles in that direction." Remo pointed west.

Chiun turned and looked in that direction for a moment, then put his hand through the metal door Remo was leaning against, as simply as if it were paper.

"When vibrations speak to you, listen," Chiun said.

Remo looked through the ragged gap in the door and saw a sign with big red Hebrew letters at the end of a long concrete reinforced hallway.

"Don't tell me what it says," said Remo.

"Danger. Radioactivity. No unauthorized personnel beyond this point," said Chiun.

"I knew it all the time," Remo said, reaching through the hole and unlocking the door.

The two moved down to the end of the hallway where an impressive-looking door attached to the danger sign blocked their way.

"Hmmm," said Remo, looking it up and down and sliding his hands over several security devices. "Looks like a special key lock and a combination lock. This looks like a time-clock mechanism and a special reinforced lock guard."

Chiun walked to the other side of the door and ripped the hinges out of the concrete wall with two rhythmic taps of his hands, taps that looked slow and gentle.

"Formidable," he said as he opened the two-foot-thick obstruction from the other side.

"Showoff," said Remo as he stared down a

166

maze-like corridor filled with sensory equipment, pressure-sensitive panels, sliding cast-iron partitions, warning lights, video-tape cameras, and more infrared devices. All inoperative.

"Delish must have switched them all off," said Remo.

Remo and Chiun moved through the hallway until they reached a last closed metal panel. Remo put his ear against it.

"I hear something," he said.

"That is good," replied Chiun. "It means you are not deaf."

"No, it means that Delish is probably in there," Remo moved back a step and was preparing to rend the door apart when it slid open.

Remo looked at Chiun, who looked back, and then they moved through the opening onto a long stairway that wound around a large circular room of dull blue metal. It gave the impression of being the insides of an upright bullet. The entire area was filled with the latest technical equipment that America could provide.

Standing in the middle of the room was Tochala Delit, tall and proud in a full S.S. uniform that he had worn under his street clothes. It was all there, from the wide red and black Nazi armband to the green, red, blue, and silver medals that gleamed on his chest.

"Who does your suits?" Remo asked.

Delit did not answer. Instead, he looked to his side where a twelve-foot-long cylinder lay. It was rounded at one end and finned at the other. The sides were rounded and smooth except for a flat, rectangular shape that stuck halfway up the tube. The rectangular thing was ticking.

167

Tochala Delit looked up and his eyes were shining.

"You are too late," he said.

Yoel Zabari could not convince the first guard to stand aside.

"How do I know you are Mr. Zabari?" asked the guard. "You have never visited us before, and Mr. Delit left instructions to allow no one else in. Not even the prime minister."

"I'm not the prime minister," shouted Zabari, "and Tochala Delit is a traitor. You know me, damn it, you have seen pictures of me. How could anyone fake this?" he stabbed at the right side of his face.

"Well, I do not know . . . ," began the guard.

"You do not know?" yelled Zabari incredulously.

That settled it for the guard. The Zeher Lahurban was probably just testing them again. Mr. Delit had said no one. No one it would be.

"I'm sorry, sir, you will have to wait for authorization."

"Damn it, that will be too late. There will not be anything to authorize if you do not let me through. And now."

Zhava Fifer saw her boss's rage mount as she sat behind the wheel of the jeep.

The guard understood that their loyalty had to be tested, but this was going a bit far.

"Sir ..." he began. Suddenly Zabari smashed him across the neck with the side of his hand.

"Drive," he said savagely as the guard spun to the ground, unconscious. "Drive, damn it!"

Zhava ground the jeep into gear and rammed

forward as Zabari pulled her dashboard automatic up.

The second perimeter guard was clicking the safety off his weapon when Zabari shot him through the leg. Zhava drove fast and straight as the second guard fell backward, spouting blood, and Zabari sprayed the entrance to the third perimeter guard shack, trying to keep the man from reaching it safely.

"Hit him," Zabari said.

"What?" cried Zhava.

"Hit him," Zabari repeated. "Try not to kill him, but hit him."

Zabari kept firing away as Zhava swerved the car and sideswiped the running guard. His body flew off the ground and somersaulted three times across the sand before finally landing in a dusty stillness.

Zabari's face was stretched tightly across his skull, and Zhava felt like crying. They tore across the plant to the nuclear area. Less than ten seconds had passed.

Remo stepped off the stairway and moved into the room that housed the atomic bomb.

"I sent away the technicians," Delit said, "and have silenced the protective devices. No alarm can be raised. The bomb cannot be neutralized. It is now only a matter of time."

Remo saw on the side of the thin rectangular bump on the bomb an electronic counter that kept tract of the passing seconds.

One hundred and eighty, one hundred and seventy-nine, one hundred and seventy-eight . . .

"Time, Herr Williams," said Delit. "That is all

that is left. After thirty years, we are down to this. Just minutes before the bomb explodes."

Chiun joined Remo beside the bomb. One hundred and sixty, one hundred and fifty-nine, one hundred and fifty-eight . . .

"It is useless to tinker with time, gentlemen. If the device is tampered with, even by myself, it will explode. And I doubt that even you, who have eluded my people for so long, could survive that."

"We'll see," said Remo. "You killed Hegez and Goldman?"

"Yes," said Delit.

"You sent those Palestinians and Markowitz after us?"

"Dorfmann? Yes."

"And you slaughtered Gavan?"

"Yes, yes, yes, I did all that. Please, Herr Williams," said the man who had been Horst Vessel, "do with me as you like. I am merely a servant of the master race."

"You do not look Korean," said Chiun, who still stood staring at the bomb and its ticking detonation device. One hundred and forty-six, one hundred and forty-five, one hundred and forty-four . . .

Delit went on as if there had been no interruption. "Germany, gentlemen. The glorious Third Reich. And now I, single-handedly, am creating the Fourth Reich."

Remo moved in. "That's your problem, pal. Don't you know that three Reichs don't correct a wrong?"

Remo's hand moved in a deceptively lazy pattern.

170

"Kill me, Herr Williams," invited Delit. "I do not care. Now or later. It makes no difference."

One hundred and thirty-two, one hundred and thirty-one, one hundred and thirty . . .

"Toe!"

Both Delit and Remo looked toward the source of that awful voice. It seemed to shake the room with its terrible pain. The ripped, broken voice came from the very bottom of Yoel Zabari's soul. He stood in the doorway of the room with Zhava Fifer.

"Toe," he cried again. "How could you do this? After what we have been through together? After all of it? Has it not touched you at all?"

Tochala Delit smiled sadly. "You Jews," he said, "you never learn. Yoel, I am only doing what the world wants me to do. Even now with your faith, you hold back the world. It wants no part of you. You have heard it through its newspapers and its United Nations votes. I have heard it. The world whispers in my ear, 'Throw your Gods away, Jews, we do not need them. We do not want them.'"

One hundred and fourteen, one hundred and thirteen, one hundred and twelve, one hundred and eleven . . .

"The world can only march forward when you and everything you represent are gone, like the dirt you sprang from and the past you represent."

"It cannot be," Zhava burst. "It will not. Our allies will avenge us."

Delit moved directly under the landing where the pair stood.

"Stupid girl," he said. "What allies? You have

no friends, only guilty enemies. Too weak, too hypocritical to say what they feel. Where were your friends during the war? Where were your allies when the six million died? Where were the Americans? Where were your own people in Jerusalem? I am killing you because the world wants you dead. You might say . . . ," Tochala Delit smiled, ". . . I am only following orders."

The room was shattered by a roar as Yoel Zabari sprang. His body hurled down upon Delit's, and the two men smashed to the floor.

Remo stood back as Zabari rose, his hands clenched tightly around Delit's neck, tears streaming down the left side of his face.

The death head grew red, then purple, then green. Even as the eyes bulged and the bloodless lips curled back on his teeth, Delit's fuzzing pupils locked onto those of Yoel Zabari.

The gritting teeth parted and a dying voice whispered, "The Nazis will not die. The world does not want them to."

Then the tongue forced its way from between the flaxen lips, the eyes rolled up, the brain died, and the heart stopped beating. Horst Vessel was dead.

Eighty-five, eighty-four, eighty-three . . .

Zabari let the corpse fall from his hands. Zhava came down the stairs and walked up to him. He looked up at her and said, "I hurt my own men for this garbage." Then he kicked the body.

Zhava Fifer wrapped her arms around Zabari and wept. Zabari looked haunted, his hands like claws. Delit lay still, the thirty years ending as he had wanted them to, in death. Remo turned to Chiun who still stood before the bomb.

Seventy-eight, seventy-seven, seventy-six . . .

Well, this is it, then, Remo thought. Technology versus the Destroyer, and no one in the world he could kill to make this bomb stop ticking. He was faster than a speeding bullet, more powerful than a locomotive and all that, but give him a machine without a plug to pull out and he was helpless.

Remo walked to Chiun and put a hand on his shoulder.

"Well, Little Father," he said gently, "do you think your ancestors will be expecting us? I'm sorry."

Chiun looked up. "Why?" he asked. "You have done nothing. Do you not know that the only use of machinery is to break down? Stand back."

And with that, the Master began to unscrew the top of the bomb.

Yoel Zabari broke out of his trance and ran forward. "Wait! What are you doing?"

Remo blocked his way. "Take it easy. What do we have to lose?"

Zabari pondered that for a second, then stood back. Zhava fell to her knees in prayer.

Chiun pulled off the top of the bomb and nothing happened. "I would have this fixed sooner," he said, "if everyone had not been talking so much." He bent down and looked into the cylinder.

Fifty-two, fifty-one, fifty . . .

"Well?" asked Remo.

"It is dark," Chiun replied.

"For the love of Jesus, Mr. Chiun," Zabari began.

"Now you've done it," said Remo.

"For Jesus?" cried Chiun, straightening. "Oh, no. We never got a day's work from Him. Now, Herod, that was something else."

Forty-five, forty-four, forty-three . . .

"Chiun, really," said Remo.

"If you read the history of Sinanju as you are supposed to, I would never have to tell you this," said Chiun.

"It's hardly the time for a history lesson, Little Father," said Remo, pointing to the bomb.

"It is never too late to learn," replied Chiun.

Thirty, twenty-nine, twenty-eight . . .

"This is what really happened to the poor wretch, Herod the Maligned. Abused by his own people, used by the Romans, he turned in pain finally to his assassin, an ancient Master of Sinanju, and said, 'I was wrong. If only I had listened to you instead of the whores and counselors who abound in this wretched land.'"

Thirteen, twelve, eleven . . .

"The ancient Master buried him in the desert."

Nine, eight, seven . . .

"Chiun, please!"

Six, five, four . . .

"To Herod the Maligned!" Chiun cried, ripping out handfuls of wires.

"It's still ticking," Zhava screamed.

Three, two, one . . . zero.

Nothing happened.

"Of course, it is still ticking," said Chiun. "I broke the bomb, not the clock."

CHAPTER SEVENTEEN

No one saw them off.

Yoel Zabari had declared undying allegiance to both Korea and America. Zhava Fifer had declared undying allegiance to Remo's body. Tochala Delit had been riddled with bullets and dropped behind enemy lines, which was not difficult since all Israel's borders were enemy lines.

But Israel still existed, so life went on as if nothing had happened. Israel nearly having been destroyed did not mean anything. Zionism was still outlawed by the UN. The Arabs were still denying the Jewish state's existence. The price of gasoline was still sixty-three cents a gallon for regular, sixty-five cents for high-test. Nothing had changed.

Yoel and Zhava went back to work, wishing Remo well and asking that he give them at least three years' notice before his next visit.

"Israel is not a place," said Chiun. "It is a state

175

of mind. The thought has not stopped, so the thought continues."

Things were not all bad, Remo learned. Smith had discovered the source of the original leak, who had revealed Remo and Chiun's mission to Israel.

"It was a simple matter of elimination," he had told Remo. "It wasn't me and it wasn't you and it wasn't Chiun so it could only have been one other person."

When Smith had mentioned the folly of ever repeating such a leak to the guilty party, the president had apologized profusely and almost choked on a peanut.

Smith had also sent instructions on to Remo to return home immediately since his job was done and Israel could safely get back to its primary national mission: staying alive.

So what the hell was Remo doing on the tea trail?

"What the hell am I doing on the tea trail?" asked Remo.

"I have done you a service, so now you must do me a service," replied Chiun.

They were walking along the centuries-old caravan trail that was lined with prayer-inscribed rocks, into the Sinai Desert.

"What other service do I owe you?" asked Remo. "You got your daytime dramas, didn't you? I sent the Norman Lear, Norman Lear letter, didn't I?"

Chiun had watched him do it, too. Only what Chiun had not seen was that Remo failed to put stamps on the envelope and had written the return address as:

176

Captain Kangaroo
CBS Television City
Hollywood, California

"So what other favor do I owe you?" Remo finished.

"Those were not services," said Chiun, "those were obligations. But do not worry, my son, I am merely looking for a sign."

"Well, hurry up, Little Father, or we'll miss the plane."

"Be calm, Remo, we could do much worse than to remain here," said Chiun.

"What is this?" retorted Remo. "Are you getting soft in the head? Where is 'this land of little beauty'? Where are the palaces of yesteryear, remember?"

"They are gone," said Chiun, "gone with the sand and returned to the earth like the bones of Herod. As it should be. The surface beauty of this land has been destroyed, but if Israel itself is destroyed, it might be best that the rest of the world be destroyed with it. Except Sinanju, of course."

"Of course," said Remo. "Quit fooling yourself. If Israel was destroyed, the world would probably turn the other way and keep going."

"Yes. Keep going to certain destruction," said Chiun, "for everything this land is, the world needs. Israel is based on the same beauty, love, and brotherhood as is Sinanju."

Remo laughed. The two places did have similarities all right. Both tended to look barren. Israel looked like a giant beachfront to Remo.

Sinanju like a mountain of crab grass littered with outhouses.

"What are you saying?" he said. "Love? Brotherhood? Sinanju? We're killers, Chiun. Sinanju is the spawning ground of the world's greatest assassins."

"Sinanju is an art before it is a place," said Chiun, his face grave. "Do you think I have just fought the atomic forces of the universe and won? I have not done this. Sinanju has done this. I am everything Sinanju is. Everything Sinanju is, is me. Israel holds the same power. It is up to the people here to tap that power."

Remo remembered the smell of sulphur and the ticking of the bomb. He remembered Delit's words and Chiun's actions. He remembered the nuclear device not exploding. But Sinanju a love nest? A monument to Brotherhood Week?

Chiun turned toward the Sinai and continued along the trail, speaking as if he had read Remo's mind.

"Yes, without our love, our brotherhood, and our home, Sinanju would just be another way of killing people. A toy to break bricks with. The world would be wise to pay heed to the lessons of the land with little visual beauty."

Remo looked out across the desert, experiencing its breathtaking view again. Just because every other landscape was a mine field and the town you passed through might not be there by the time you got back didn't mean that one could still not learn to love the place. Remo thought about Zhava and the flowers.

"There," came Chiun's voice, interrupting Remo's dreams. Remo turned and saw the

178

Korean kneel by a rock, then leap to his feet and move quickly across the desert.

Remo ran past the other prayer-inscribed rocks until he came to the one Chiun had been by.

"Praise be to Herod the Wonderful," Chiun's voice drifted across the sand, "a fine, noble, honest man whose word even after centuries is as good as gold."

The rock had been inscribed with the letters, "C-H-I-U-N." Remo ran after the aged Korean.

"It is the sign I have been promised by the ancient chapters in the Book of Sinanju," Remo heard. "Come quickly into the desert, my son."

Remo plowed after Chiun's diminishing shape. "Where are we going?" Remo called into the wind.

"We are going to collect a debt," answered the Oriental's voice.

The dust rose in Remo's face from the speed of the Korean. Remo shut his eyes and kept running until he felt the grittiness disappear from his senses.

When he opened his eyes again, he was standing with Chiun before a small cave, seemingly etched out of the sand and rock. Chiun smiled at him knowingly, then went inside. Remo followed, bending over to fit through the small opening.

"Ah," said Chiun, "you see?"

Inside the cave was a small room lit by a series of canals cut into the solid rock. Atop a thick rug was a skeleton wrapped in royal robes and wearing jewelry. Before the body were two heaps of gold. The walls were lined with silk.

"Friend of yours?" asked Remo.

"Herod is a man of his word," said Chiun.

179

"*Was* a man of his word," replied Remo. "This can't be Herod. He was buried in Herodonia." Remo looked at the mummified bones and the diamonds and ruby encrustations, then at the expression on Chiun's face. "Wasn't he?"

Chiun felt it unnecessary to reply. "We will take the gold that belongs to Sinanju," he said, instead. "Come." He handed Remo a silken bag.

"Why me?" said Remo. "You should pick up your own pay."

"This is the service that you owe," said Chiun. "You should be honored that I am allowing you to glimpse the innermost workings of Sinanju."

"Yeah, collecting money," said Remo, wondering how the hell he might get a silken bag filled with gold through customs. "Lucky me."

After the gold was secure, Chiun took the sack and walked to the mouth of the cave. As Remo joined him, the Oriental turned for a last look at the skeleton that had once been an emperor of one of the strongest empires that had ever existed.

"So it is. So it was. So it always shall be. Poor Herod the Maligned. The Book of Sinanju states, 'A human being is here today—in the grave tomorrow.'"

Remo turned to the reigning Master of Sinanju and remembered where he had heard that before. And from whose lips.

"That's funny, Chiun," he said. "You don't look Jewish."

THE EXECUTIONER
by Don Pendleton

#1:	WAR AGAINST THE MAFIA	(17-024-3, $3.50)
#2:	DEATH SQUAD	(17-025-1, $3.50)
#3:	BATTLE MASK	(17-026-X, $3.50)
#4:	MIAMI MASSACRE	(17-027-8, $3.50)
#5:	CONTINENTAL CONTRACT	(17-028-6, $3.50)
#6:	ASSAULT ON SOHO	(17-029-4, $3.50)
#7:	NIGHTMARE IN NEW YORK	(17-066-9, $3.50)
#8:	CHICAGO WIPEOUT	(17-067-7, $3.50)
#9:	VEGAS VENDETTA	(17-068-5, $3.50)
#10:	CARIBBEAN KILL	(17-069-3, $3.50)
#11:	CALIFORNIA HIT	(17-070-7, $3.50)
#12:	BOSTON BLITZ	(17-071-5, $3.50)
#13:	WASHINGTON I.O.U.	(17-172-X, $3.50)
#14:	SAN DIEGO SIEGE	(17-173-8, $3.50)
#15:	PANIC IN PHILLY	(17-174-6, $3.50)
#16:	SICILIAN SLAUGHTER	(17-175-4, $3.50)
#17:	JERSEY GUNS	(17-176-2, $3.50)
#18:	TEXAS STORM	(17-177-0, $3.50)

Available wherever paperbacks are sold, or order direct from the Publisher. Send cover price plus 50¢ per copy for mailing and handling to Pinnacle Books, Dept. 17- 295, 475 Park Avenue South, New York, N.Y. 10016. Residents of New York, New Jersey and Pennsylvania must include sales tax. DO NOT SEND CASH.

WARBOTS by G. Harry Stine

#5 OPERATION HIGH DRAGON (17-159, $3.95)
Civilization is under attack! A "virus program" has been injected into America's polar-orbit military satellites by an unknown enemy. The only motive can be the preparation for attack against the free world. The source of "infection" is traced to a barren, storm-swept rock-pile in the southern Indian Ocean. Now, it is up to the forces of freedom to search out and destroy the enemy. With the aid of their robot infantry—the Warbots—the Washington Greys mount Operation High Dragon in a climactic battle for the future of the free world.

#6 THE LOST BATTALION (17-205, $3.95)
Major Curt Carson has his orders to lead his Warbot-equipped Washington Greys in a search-and-destroy mission in the mountain jungles of Borneo. The enemy: a strongly entrenched army of Shiite Muslim guerrillas who have captured the Second Tactical Battalion, threatening them with slaughter. As allies, the Washington Greys have enlisted the Grey Lotus Battalion, a mixed-breed horde of Japanese jungle fighters. Together with their newfound allies, the small band must face swarming hordes of fanatical Shiite guerrillas in a battle that will decide the fate of Southeast Asia and the security of the free world.

#7 OPERATION IRON FIST (17-253, $3.95)
Russia's centuries-old ambition to conquer lands along its southern border erupts in a savage show of force that pits a horde of Soviet-backed Turkish guerrillas against the freedom-loving Kurds in their homeland high in the Caucasus Mountains. At stake: the rich oil fields of the Middle East. Facing certain annihilation, the valiant Kurds turn to the robot infantry of Major Curt Carson's "Ghost Forces" for help. But the brutal Turks far outnumber Carson's desperately embattled Washington Greys, and on the blood-stained slopes of historic Mount Ararat, the high-tech warriors of tomorrow must face their most awesome challenge yet!

Available wherever paperbacks are sold, or order direct from the Publisher. Send cover price plus 50¢ per copy for mailing and handling to Pinnacle Books, Dept.17-295, 475 Park Avenue South, New York, N.Y. 10016. Residents of New York, New Jersey and Pennsylvania must include sales tax. DO NOT SEND CASH.

PINNACLE'S FINEST IN SUSPENSE
AND ESPIONAGE

OPIUM   (17-077, $4.50)
by Tony Cohan

Opium! The most alluring and dangerous substance known to man. The ultimate addiction, ensnaring all in its lethal web. A nerve-shattering odyssey into the perilous heart of the international narcotics trade, racing from the beaches of Miami to the treacherous twisting alleyways of the Casbah, from the slums of Paris to the teeming Hong Kong streets to the war-torn jungles of Vietnam.

TRUK LAGOON   (17-121, $3.95)
by Mitchell Sam Rossi

Two bizarre destinies inseparably linked over forty years unlease a savage storm of violence, treachery, and greed on a tropic island paradise. The most incredible covert operation in military history is about to be uncovered—a lethal mystery hidden for decades amid the wreckage of war far beneath the Truk Lagoon.

LAST JUDGMENT   (17-114, $4.50)
by Richard Hugo

Seeking vengeance for the senseless murders of his brother, sister-in-law, and their three children, former S.A.S. agent James Ross plunges into the perilous world of fanatical terrorism to prevent a centuries-old vision of the Apocalypse from becoming reality, as the approaching New Year threatens to usher in mankind's dreaded Last Judgment.

THE JASMINE SLOOP   (17-113, $3.95)
by Frank J. Kenmore

A man of rare and lethal talents, Colin Smallpiece has crammed ten lifetimes into his twenty-seven years. Now, drawn from his peaceful academic life into a perilous web of intrigue and assassination, the ex-intelligence operative has set off to locate a U.S. senator who has vanished mysteriously from the face of the Earth.

Available wherever paperbacks are sold, or order direct from the Publisher. Send cover price plus 50¢ per copy for mailing and handling to Pinnacle Books, Dept.17-295, 475 Park Avenue South, New York, N.Y. 10016. Residents of New York, New Jersey and Pennsylvania must include sales tax. DO NOT SEND CASH.

MYSTIC REBEL by Ryder Syvertsen

MYSTIC REBEL   (17-104, $3.95)
It was duty that first brought CIA operative Bart Lasker to the mysterious frozen mountains of Tibet. But a deeper obligation made him remain behind, disobeying orders to wage a personal war against the brutal Red Chinese oppressors.

MYSTIC REBEL II   (17-079, $3.95)
Conscience first committed CIA agent Bart Lasker to Tibet's fight for deliverance from the brutal yoke of Red Chinese oppression. But a strange and terrible power bound the unsuspecting American to the mysterious kingdom—freeing the Western avenger from the chains of mortality, transforming him from mere human to the MYSTIC REBEL!

MYSTIC REBEL III   (17-141, $3.95)
At the bidding of the Dalai Lama, the Mystic Rebel must return to his abandoned homeland to defend a newborn child. The infant's life-spark is crucial to the survival of the ancient mountain people—but forces of evil have vowed that the child shall die at birth.

MYSTIC REBEL IV   (17-232, $3.95)
Nothing short of death at the hands of his most dreaded enemies—the Bonpo magicians, worshippers of the Dark One—will keep the legendary warrior from his chosen destiny—a life or death struggle in the labyrinthine depths of the Temple of the Monkey God, where the ultimate fate of a doomed world hangs in the balance!

Available wherever paperbacks are sold, or order direct from the Publisher. Send cover price plus 50¢ per copy for mailing and handling to Pinnacle Books, Dept.17-295, 475 Park Avenue South, New York, N.Y. 10016. Residents of New York, New Jersey and Pennsylvania must include sales tax. DO NOT SEND CASH.